MY FIGHT

MICKY'S GYM

ELLA TAYLOR

Paula
Happy Reading
xoxo
Ella Taylor

LG Publishing Partners, LLC

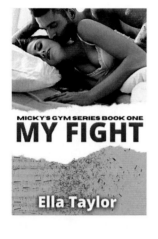

MICKY'S GYM SERIES BOOK ONE

MY FIGHT

Ella Taylor

When love and survival collide, can a fighter find the strength to fight for both?

After escaping an abusive relationship, MacKenna returns to her hometown and fights to protect herself while also dealing with her long-repressed feelings for her brother's best friend, Ryan, who has been in love with her since they were teenagers.

MacKenna:

I left my hometown to chase my dreams of becoming a songwriter in Boston, but I never imagined I would find myself in an abusive relationship. Growing up in a family of MMA fighters, I never thought I'd be in this situation. But I gained the courage to leave, and now, I'm back home with my brothers. This story is about a strong young woman who doesn't need a man to protect her. But when my ex reappears, I'll do whatever it takes to keep myself safe. Will love prevail, or will my past keep me from moving forward?

Ryan:

I have been best friends with MacKenna's brothers for as long as I can remember, and I have been in love with her since we were teenagers. I never had the courage to tell her my feelings, especially after my mother's murder, but MacKenna's family saved me. Now, she's back home, and I can no longer hide my feelings. Will MacKenna's brothers keep us apart, or will we find a way to be together? I want to be the one who helps her see the good in a man again, but will it be enough to heal the wounds of her past?

"My Fight" is a powerful and emotional story about love, survival, and the strength to fight for both.

If you or a loved one is a victim of domestic abuse and need to talk, please call 1(800)799-SAFE anytime in the United States. It's free and confidential. Or go to www.thehotline.org

MICKY'S GYM

My Fight
Micky's Gym
COPYRIGHT©2023
Ella Taylor
Cover Design by Wren Taylor

Published in the United States of America by:

DLG Publishing Partners
PO Box 17674
San Antonio, TX 78217
www.DLGPublishingPartners.com

To my Husband, Scott. Thank you for your love, support, patience, and strength. Thank you for your smile that makes me smile. To my two beautiful daughters Madison and Kennedy: Thank you for making every day the best day!

ACKNOWLEDGMENTS

A couple of years ago, my husband bought me a Kindle after the most important man in my life, the man who raised me and guided me to be the person I am today, passed away. I threw myself into reading and realized how much better reading the written word and creating the visuals in my head of the storylines were so much better than turning on the television hanging on the wall.

It is because of you, Scott, that I began to write—because of you, I followed through and finished. When you told me to get it out to the world, I laughed, but your push gave me the strength to try. And now, because of your love, patience, strength, and support, I am moving on to the next book. You have always been and will always be, the love of my life.

Madison and Kennedy, thank you for giving me quiet time to write, especially when all you wanted to do was blast a Marvel movie!

Lissa, you took the time to read "My Fight" and

give me your honest opinion and when you begged for more of the story, it inspired me to sit down and write the next part of Mackenna' and Ryan's live together.

AUTHOR'S NOTE

To my readers,

Thank you for taking a chance on me and reading my books. It means the world to me.

"My Fight" is a powerful and emotional story about love, survival, and the strength to fight for both.

If you or a loved one is a victim of domestic abuse and need to talk, please call 1(800)799-SAFE anytime in the United States. It's free and confidential. Or go to www.thehotline.org

Thank you for reading "My Fight,"

Ella Taylor

PROLOGUE

At least it's not raining anymore.

Anyone who grew up here knew a heavy rain-
storm was normal weather in Florida. Now that the
rain had stopped, allowing the clouds to part and
make way for the shining sun to shine, the tempera-
tures had risen.

I took one last glance around the walls of the
home I grew up in.

Memories flooded my mind. Overgrown weeds
and grass hid the backyard. During my childhood, it
was where my brothers and I had played, and it was,
most importantly where I sat with my mom.

The floorboards creak a little more underfoot,
showing the age of the house. As I turn to the front
door, I see my daddy waiting for me.

"Your car's all loaded up," Daddy said in a quiet voice.

He may be smiling on the outside, but I know him. The man's heartbroken that I've chosen to leave home and head North for College.

"Thanks, Daddy, I'm coming." I smiled, then I walked toward him.

He's waiting for me by the door. Together, we exit the front entry and head down the porch steps. A tear trickles over my cheek, and I swipe it.

"It's not too late to stay. We have plenty of good schools here." Daddy wraps his arm around my shoulder and pulls me close.

Glancing at him, I didn't see what most people saw.

Yes, he's tall and all muscle. Some would say scary but not me. All I saw was a protective teddy bear. And right now, he's looking at me with a tear in his blue eyes not wanting to let his little girl go.

My green eyes met his. "Daddy, I'm going. I'll be back before you even miss me."

"I already miss you, my sweet girl." He uses his thumb to wipe one of my tears away.

I had already said my goodbyes early this morning, and now it was just my favorite guy here and me. It was so hard to say goodbye earlier, but it's killing my heart saying it to my dad.

This big, strong man standing here holds me tighter than he has ever before in my life, making my heart physically hurt.

How am I going to get in my car and drive away?

His hands cup my cheeks, holding my face.

"Baby girl." his voice hoarse, "You go and show the world what you're made of. You share your voice with them, and I swear, I'll be right here just as proud as I've always been of you."

He swipes another tear from my cheek with his thumb.

"You are beautiful." His voice cracks. "You're smart. My baby girl is amazing . . . I love you, my sweetheart."

That's it. My daddy's words officially broke my heart. *I can't take anymore.*

My knees buckle, but my daddy holds me tight, wrapping his big arms around me. He embraces me until my legs stabilize. But even then, he doesn't let go.

Once my heart beats normally again, I loosened my hold.

"I love you," he whispers in my ear, still holding on. "I'm right here whenever you decide to come home."

Without another word, he releases his grip, turns around, and then walks me to the driver side door.

He opens the door, and I told myself onto the seat. I gaze at him again.

"I love you, Daddy. My voice shakes.

A tear runs down his cheek.

Once last glance out the car window, I burn his image to memory, blow him a kiss, then start the ignition.

With the sun shining overhead, I shift the car into drive and pulled away from all that I know and love: my home, my family, and my daddy.

My journey of independence starts now!

1

MACKENNA

"Mackenna, will you grab that group of guys at the end of the bar?" Jeff asked.

Jeff is my bartending partner in this shithole of a bar. I've worked here and with Jeff for over a year, just before I graduated college. Jeff is still in college; he graduates this spring. He was born and raised here in Massachusetts. I came here over 4 years ago from my home in Orlando. I could not wait to get here. I had dreamed of moving to Massachusetts when I was in junior high and learned there was more than one season.

Jeff is handsome, and the girls who would come out to the bar always hung out to watch him behind the bar. He was tall *but* not too tall, probably just under six feet, with toned features but not huge muscles. It was his smile that grabbed girls. He was always smiling that big smile that showed off a cute dimple in his right cheek. He always has a sparkle in his big brown eyes. Like he was happy to be here. *My eyes never sparkled like that.*

Jeff put his hand through his dark brown hair that always fell over his eyes and yelled again . . . "Hey Kenna grab those guys at the end of the bar for me?"

"No problem, let me just finish getting these guys their beers, and I will head down," I yelled back to him.

As I put a cup under the draft, I glanced down at the end of the bar to a group of four guys and yelled, "I'll be right down." I skimmed over their features quickly and noticed the one wearing a white polo giving me a wink. As I turned away and grabbed a second glass, I rolled my eyes. *Who wears a polo to a dive bar*, I thought? This place was a shithole. Most guys wore a t-shirt and jeans here.

I handed the two guys their draft beers and grabbed the money they handed over. I smiled and said a quick "thank you."

"You can keep the rest" one of them said. I smiled and in a loud voice spoke over the music and crowd, "thanks for the tip, guys."

I threw the money into my tip jar that was located to the left of the register. Jeff's tip jar was located on the right. I wiped my hands on the wet towel that hung by the register. Pouring drinks your hands would constantly get sticky and touching people's money was just *gross*!

This bar was always busy. It was located between two colleges and because we served some crappy beer on draft it was cheap, and the college kids could afford it. It was truly a shithole. This place had two small windows, the walls were concrete with a huge Irish flag painted on one of them, on another wall was a shamrock painted with the name of the bar O'Donnell's. The bar was stained a dark mahogany with bar stools lined all the way down.

The Shelving on the wall behind the bar held the hard liquor along with the register and our tip jars. There was a television up on the wall in two of the corners. The volume was muted so no one really paid attention to it unless there was a Red Sox game, Bruin's game or a Patriots game. The DJ was in the far corner away from the bar. There was no need for a dance floor people just danced in the middle of the room. The lighting was dark which made just about everyone look good if you had a few drinks in you.

As I walked to the end of the bar to greet the four guys that were waiting, my eyes scanned their appearance. I assumed they were frat boys from one of the colleges. They were standing there all wearing polo shirts. They looked like they came from one of the Ivy league colleges on the other side of the city.

Each one of them had that look of *'my shit doesn't stink, and I live off of mommy and daddy's money.'*

I made my way down the bar with a fake smile on my face wondering how much longer until I could yell, "Last call."

I stared directly at the *shithead* in the middle of the group. The one who gave me the wink. With the sweetest voice I could muster up, I said, "Hi, boys. What can I get you?" Still looking at the middle one, I gave him a cute little wink.

I knew what he would do before he even did it, and as I expected, he slowly moved his eyes down my small five-foot-four-inch frame, stopping first at my average size chest and slowly down my slender stomach that was currently exposed and showing my naval.

Then his gaze moved on to my hips, which were a little wider. Once his eyes reached my hips, he slowly brought his eyes back up, meeting my green eyes. I knew I was not horrible looking, but I was no drop-dead gorgeous girl either. I was an average-looking girl with wavy red hair.

Growing up, I hated the waves in my hair. I always tried to straighten it, but I was no good with a hair straightener. I would always burn my fingers or my scalp, so I said, "fuck it" and threw it in the trash. I had nice skin with a good complexion. I moisturized every morning and night. I was not pale but nor was I tan. I had deep green eyes that I got from my mother. Actually, I looked just like her. I was her mini-me. I wore a 'C' bra cup which was pretty good for being so short. I had a toned stomach and toned legs from working out. I wore very little makeup, only mascara and lip gloss. I was girly but not too girly.

Once the asshole was satisfied with ogling me, he stated, "Four Jager bombs." *Yup, he's a total douche.* "And four Guinness."

"You got it! Hang tight, handsome." I knew how to play the game to get the tips!

I grabbed four shot glasses, the Jägermeister, and Red Bull to make the Jager bombs. As I poured out the shots, I took a glimpse down the bar at Jeff, who was at the other end waiting on some cute girls.

He glanced over and gave me that stupid grin he liked to give.

That was his way of saying, *ha-ha, better you then me waiting on those assholes.*

God, he was a pain in my ass sometimes. Whom was I kidding, Jeff was a pain in my ass most nights?

I nodded at him, which was my way of saying, *Fuck you, buddy!*

As I finished making the Jager bombs I glimpsed down at the four guys waiting, with their stupid polo shirts, smiling like I could not wait to be near them again.

Ugh, how much longer until last call.

I brought my wrist up and peaked at my watch and smiled . . . only thirty more minutes until I could yell, 'last call.'

I didn't usually glance at my watch to see if the night was almost over. Most nights went by quickly, and to be honest, I usually enjoyed my job. I liked that the bar was always busy, and I could socialize with the regulars. They were good tippers most of the time.

And it helped that the DJ played good music that I could get lost in.

Tonight, though, all I wanted to do was curl up into a ball and go to sleep. Too much had been weighing on me lately, and I'd not been sleeping well.

Once the shots were poured, I handed them over along with the red bulls and then move to get the four Guinness on draft. I could feel myself losing patience. I wasn't in the mood for any more crap tonight, but time was dragging, and so were my feet. I shook my head in hopes that I could shake this bad attitude, so I could get through the rest of the night.

"It is almost over. I can make it," I said to myself.

After handing over the four drafts, I reached out for the shithead's credit card that I'm sure mommy and daddy were funding.

Yup, I still have a bad attitude.

Inserting the card into the credit card machine, I secretly hoped it would decline just so I could embarrass the guy.

My god, I'm a total bitch tonight. I hoped the customers weren't feeling my attitude!

Accepted, the receipt printed, and I handed it over with a pen for him to sign. Before he could finish, I turned to the next group. A cute group of girls who just barely turned twenty-one. You could always tell the ones who just turned twenty-one. They always said their drink order quietly, and I usually had to ask them to repeat themselves. They, of course, ordered a fruity cocktail. It was always a fruity cocktail. Most were too young to know a good drink.

I went along making drinks and minding my own business. Then, I heard music to my ear.

"Last call," Jeff called out from the other end of the bar.

Ugh, this night will just not end.

The guy with the mommy and daddy trust fund held up the receipt I had handed him to sign.

I put one finger up, signaling just a minute. As I made my way down the bar, taking orders and making drinks, I could feel his eyes on me. A few minutes later, I reached out to grab the receipt, but the asshole pulled it back.

A smile hit my lips but not my eyes because what else could I do at that moment? Well, I knew what I wanted to do, kick him in the balls, but I was behind a bar, and it would get me fired.

But I was sure Jeff would get a kick out of it, though!

Mr. Polo smiled. It was as if he thought that what he was doing was cute. When the idiot handed me the receipt, I noticed a very generous tip.

I guessed I was hiding my bad attitude well. *Yea. Go me!*

"Sweetheart, how about you give me your number so we can get together sometime?" Mr. Polo asked.

That would be a big fat no!

There was no way this guy was getting my number, which was out of the question. "No thanks. I've a polo already at home," I answered.

As I turned away, my eyes meet Jeff's. He gave me those eyes that said, 'sorry.'

That's what it was like for us at the bar. We spoke in smiles and eye contact. I could read him like a book. He wasn't saying sorry to me for waiting on the douchebag, he was saying sorry because I already had a polo at home.

Jeff knew exactly what the polo comment meant. Just like I could read Jeff, he could do the same. He was just as good at reading me. There was no sense in dwelling, so I moved along and continued to hustle to make as many drinks as I could before the end of the night. The more drinks I made, the more tips I'd make, and I needed those tips.

By this time of the night, my feet were on fire. They hurt so bad. I never wore the right shoes. I knew in order to make good tips, I had to dress the part. I was wearing skinny jeans with holes in the knees, cute brown ankle boots that I found on sale, and I had a white t-shirt with the bars clover logo on it tied at the stomach. My socks were wet from all the spilled booze, and of course, my cute boots were not waterproof. My wavy red hair was down and reached my lower back. It was all sweaty at the nape of my neck from all the heat the packed bar was giving off.

I'm so done for the night.

The night was finally coming to an end, and I was watching customers slowly exit out and into the streets. There were a few people left finishing up their drinks, but Jeff and I begin cleaning up. Jeff was grabbing empty cups, and I was wiping down the liquor bottle that were lining the shelves.

Once the last group made their way outside, I exhaled quickly.

"This night sucked!" I climbed from behind the bar and dropped onto one of the barstools with my feet screaming, "Thank you."

Jeff rolled his eyes and chuckled. "Tonight wasn't that bad."

"I'm so tired. I thought tonight would never end, and my poor little feet are killing me," I said.

"You better keep those fucking feet in those boots. It already smells like shit in here. Now get your ass up and help me. The sooner we finish, the sooner we can get our asses out of here and sleep," Jeff stated with a stupid grin popping that cute dimple on his cheek.

I knew he was right, but that didn't stop me from being childish and sticking my tongue out at him as I stepped up off the stool, silently cursing these stupid boots. I grabbed the spray bottle and another rag, then started cleaning the bar.

Jeff continued to grab more trash. We move along like we did every night. The music was done, and it was quiet except for my humming.

"That's nice. Something new?" Jeff asked.

"What?" I was so busy in my own head I didn't hear what Jeff said.

"What you're humming. Is that something new you are working on?" Jeff asked.

"No, nothing new. Just something I wrote a long time ago. Actually, I haven't written anything in a while. Haven't been very motivated lately," I replied.

"I wonder why. Kenna, could it be the shitty polo you have? That one should be donated to goodwill." Jeff chuckled.

"Ugh, Jeff, stop. Let's just finish so we can get out of here," I said with complete exhaustion in my voice.

"Sure," he stated flatly.

Once the cleaning was done at least done enough for the cleaning crew to come in and finish up in the morning. I put both hands on the bar and let out a deep cleansing breath. I can feel Jeff come up behind me and reaches his arms around my waist to hug me and slaps a kiss on my cheek.

Jeff spoke in a whisper, "I'm sorry for what I said. I love you. You know that. I just worry about you and want you to be okay."

I smiled even though my back was to him, and he couldn't see it. I put my hands on his arms that were wrapped around me and told him, "It's okay. Everything will be okay."

He slapped another kiss to my cheek and then spun me around with one hand while grabbing my tip jar with his other. "Let's see what we made tonight."

I dragged my burning feet to the same barstool I was sitting on not long ago. I emptied the jar and started counting my tips. Tonight was a pretty good night considering it was a Thursday. I split my tips into two piles.

When Jeff came around, I smiled at him and handed him one of my tip piles. That was a little less than half of what I made tonight.

Jeff being Jeff, spoke with a smile that said, *'I will take care of it.'*

I wasn't worried. I trusted Jeff. I knew he would take care of the tip money I handed him. Jeff was my best friend here. To be honest, he was one of my only friends here. When I moved to Massachusetts, I didn't know anyone, and because I kept to myself a lot. I didn't make many friends. Jeff was a talented writer. I think that was why we hit it off and became so close.

Not only was he a talented writer, but he also had a talent for reading people. He knew exactly how I was feeling without me saying a word. I knew he was worried about me. I knew he wanted to help me. I also knew I could not get him any more involved than he was already. He was already doing too much with me, giving him some of my tip money every night. There was no way I would drag him into any more then he was already.

"Let's get out of this shithole," Jeff stated.

He grabbed my arm and dragged me off the stool, then to the back room located down the hall that had the bathrooms and into a room filled with kegs and booze. I took my coat and bag from one of the hooks that hung on the back of the door.

It was late September in New England, which meant the afternoons were warm, but once the sun went down, it got chilly.

I put on my light coat. I loved this coat, another thing I got on sale last season. It was a cute black peacoat that landed at my hips. It wasn't heavy. It was made out of nylon which blocked out the wind. I buttoned it up and swung my cross-body bag over my shoulder. It took me only a week after moving here to get a crossbody bag. I saw two women's purses taken right out of their hands. I knew no asshole was getting my bag! I went out and got my own crossbody purse that week.

Jeff and I each grabbed a couple of bags of trash that were at the back door and brought them to the dumpster located outside the backdoor in the alleyway. He locked up, and we walked to the street. Jeff lived just two blocks from the alley, my car was always parked around the corner, but we would take a right out of the alley. Every night Jeff would turn right and walk me to my car, and every night, we would have the same conversation.

"I can make it around the corner to where my car is parked. I can take care of myself, you know," I said sternly.

"Oh, I know, but it is the only time I get you to myself." Jeff smiled.

Every night I would laugh and smack him in the chest.

"Oof." Jeff would fake hurt and place a hand on his chest.

I could see my car parked under the streetlight in the dingy parking lot. My 2010 blue Toyota Camry. I bought this car as soon as I got my acceptance letter to college. It was the first big purchase I ever made. It may not have been much, but it was mine. That car brought me here packed full of all my stuff. It was good on gas. It was reliable and got me where I needed to be for the last five years. This car was my everything. It held all my thoughts.

God knows I spent so much time thinking.

"All right, it's getting cold. Get in that shit show you call a car and lock the doors." Jeff grabbed my chin, lifted my face to his, and added, "Get home."

Jeff ended each night we worked together like this.

He stood next to me by my car. "Be safe."

I gave him a hug, smiled against his chest, and said, "Always."

But I knew that spoken word was a lie.

Once I started the ignition, I blew into my hands and rubbed them together. It was getting cold, colder than normal for the end of September. I put the car into drive and pulled out of the parking lot, turning left to head back to my place. I rubbed my eyes, completely exhausted, and wiggled my toes because they hurt so badly. I couldn't wait to take my boots off and let my feet breathe.

It took me close to twenty minutes to get home. I hit every single red light. Of course, that would be my luck tonight. If I were lucky and hit every green light, it would only take me ten minutes. Finally, I was pulling into my parking lot behind a group of four buildings. I lived in the second building on the second floor. They weren't much to look at, just a worn brick building that had storefronts on the front side and about four apartments in each building. We all had our own designated parking spot.

As I was pulling in, I noticed the car that was parked in mine. "God damn it," I snapped. I slowly drove to the furthest end of the parking lot, had a few extra spots, and pulled into one. I hated parking over here. There was no light, so I was always nervous getting out of my car. I was no fool; I knew I lived in a bad neighborhood, but it was all I could afford.

As soon as I shut my car off, I took a look around before getting out to make sure no one was around. It was very late, or should I say very early morning. There were only a few people from the building hanging out around a trash can they had a fire in, drinking, smoking, and I'm sure laughing about some stupid story someone was telling. I made my way to the back stairway that led up to the second floor. I glanced over and smiled at my neighbors because, well, I was a good neighbor!

Putting my keys into the lock on my apartment door that was located on the left of the stairway, I took a deep breath and turned the key and then the knob to the door. I quietly entered my apartment, placing my keys onto the small side table I had by my door, and turned on the table lamp to let in a little light. I walked down the entryway, stopping at the kitchen to grab a water from the fridge.

My kitchen was tiny, with only a few cabinets and barely any counter space, but it had what I needed, well, except for a dishwasher. That was fine; it wasn't like I cooked gourmet meals, mostly ramen, grilled cheese, and a few other quick meals. I downed half the bottle of water I grabbed, feeling better about having something cool down my throat after working all night.

I made my way to the living room if you would call it that. It was almost as small as the kitchen. I had a small brown loveseat against one of the walls with a fluffy yellow throw blanket thrown over it. On the other side was a small television that sat on a stand. I peeked over to the corner of the small room, and there sat my prized possession, my guitar. I hadn't picked it up in a few weeks. I just didn't have it in me.

Tonight, though, I walked myself over to it and picked it up. I turned to the loveseat and plopped down. I held it in my arms, just feeling it. One single tear ran down my cheek, and I wiped it away.

Nope, not going to cry.

As I put the guitar down carefully, I cursed myself for even letting one tear out and for still having these damn boots on. I leaned over and pulled them off my feet, along with my soaked socks. I moved my feet around to try and get rid of the pain. After a minute of letting my feet breathe, I glanced back at my guitar and lifted it back into my arms. I moved my fingers across the strings and looked around the small room, landing on the picture that hung on my wall, the same wall my television was on.

The picture was an 8x10 framed photo of me in the middle, with two huge guys on either side of me squeezing me so tight. They were both huge, one six feet three inches and the other six feet four inches. They both had really short black hair, so short they were almost bald. The one on the right of me had a sleeve tattoo, and the other was tattooed almost anyplace there was skin. Both arms and legs—you couldn't see the ones on his chest from the grey t-shirt he was wearing with black gym shorts.

You would think I was in pain with how much they were squeezing me, but there I was with the biggest, brightest smile on my face. That smile brought out the dimple on my left cheek. You always knew when I was truly happy, that damn dimple would pop out. Those guys in the photo were my home, my protectors, my brothers.

We were all close in age. Conor and Finn were my older twin brothers, now twenty-six years old, and I was now twenty-four. I spent my childhood following my brothers and their best friend Ryan around, making their life hell, always telling on them when they were doing something they should not.

In return, they made my life hell by scaring any boy remotely interested in me away. Because of them, I left for college with no boy experience. Even though I was a huge pain in their ass, we loved each other, and they always took care of me.

Ugh, I miss them right now.

I grabbed my phone from my bag and opened a text message, adding both Conor and Finn to it.

> Me: Hi, Con.

> Me: Hi, Finn. I miss you.

IT TOOK ABOUT TEN SECONDS FOR A REPLY.

> Finn: Are you okay?

> Conor: I miss you too!

> Me: I'm okay, Finn.

> Me: I just got home from work and am tired.

> Me: I just wanted to let you know I missed you.

> Conor: Did you watch Ry's fight last weekend?

> Me: Shit. I forgot he had a fight.

> Me: It has been a crazy few weeks.

> Me: How did it go?

> Finn: I can't believe you missed it.

> Finn: You never miss a fight.

Conor: Fuck that.

Conor: If you want to know, check the highlights.

Conor: Or ask Ry yourself.

Me: Ugh. I'm sorry.

Me: I will text Ry now.

Releasing a deep breath, I sighed, then I scrolled through my phone, rereading the texts.

2

MACKENNA

Ryan was Conor's best friend since kindergarten, and Finn had just joined the friendship. Ryan was a mixed martial arts fighter. Both my brothers trained him in our family gym. My dad, long ago, was a fighter and was known for holding back-alley fights. He set them up, negotiated the fights, and took bets. Completely illegal, but if you had asked him if he regretted doing it, he would have said no way; it brought him to my mother. My mother went to a fight one night with a few of her girlfriends. My dad saw her, and he used to say that was it. He was in love.

She eventually got him to stop the illegal fights and gambling. Instead, he opened a gym. It started small, but he stuck with it and grew to bring on legitimate fighters. Conor and Ryan were always there growing up, and when they became teenagers, they started to train. Conor was never interested in headlining a fight; he always liked training the fighter. Finn, on the other hand, loved to be in the octagon. When Dad passed last year, they took over the gym and all the fighters at the gym.

I did a quick search on my phone and easily found the highlights from the fight that was on pay-per-view last Saturday night. Ryan was a good fighter. He was in the light heavyweight division. Ryan was six-foot-three inches and usually weighed around two hundred twelve pounds.

Ryan had trained with my family since he was fifteen and joined Conor and Finn. Both my brothers trained Ry. I was not surprised when the highlights showed Ryan winning in the second round by knockout. Ryan was quick on his feet and knew how to throw a punch.

Opening a new text message, I quickly typed out a text to Ryan.

> Me: Hey, Ry, I just watched the highlights.

> Me: Congrats on the win.

I wanted to say more, but I couldn't bring myself to type what I really wanted to say. Instead, I sent a quick congratulations and put my phone down on the coffee table. My apartment was dark, but I had very little, so I made my way over to the bathroom in the dark, shut the door, and hit the light switch.

Glancing at myself in the mirror, ugh, I looked exhausted. I had bags under my eyes, and my cheeks were sunken in. I had lost some weight from being emotionally withdrawn. I quickly washed my face and brushed my teeth. I had a t-shirt hanging on the door hook. I undressed and threw the t-shirt over my head and through my arms.

I took one last look at myself in the mirror and shut the light. My bedroom was right beside the bathroom. The door was closed, so I opened it and walked over to the left side of the queen bed. It was about the only thing that fit in the room. I had one small end table that fit on the right side of the bed and another small dresser on the opposite wall next to—you guessed it—a small closet.

Slowly, I slipped under the covers and lay on my back, looking up at the ceiling. I didn't move when a leg draped over mine and an arm over my chest. I didn't make a sound, just continued to stare at the ceiling, wishing my eyes would close and I would get some sleep.

"You're home later than usual."

Ugh, shit, I woke him up.

"I'm sorry, I didn't mean to wake you. It was a busy night, and it took a little while to get the stragglers out and get the bar cleaned up," I whispered.

"You were that busy tonight, really?" he asked again.

I knew that meant he didn't believe me. He thought I was lying to him.

"Yes, it was busy. I'm sorry. I'm late. I really didn't mean to wake you," I whispered again.

That was it. He said nothing else. After about a minute, I heard his breathing even out and knew he had fallen back to sleep. I, on the other hand, was wide awake with the weight from his leg and arm holding me down.

The way the sunlight was entering my bedroom and directly at my bed, I rolled over, knowing it was only a little after six thirty in the morning.

"Brad, it's around six thirty. Do you need to get up for work?" I whispered.

His eyes flickered a little before he opened his eyes, looking directly at me. When I met Brad, I thought he had the prettiest brown eyes. Now they just looked dark and mean.

"Ugh, yes, I need to get up and moving. My dad

has a meeting with an investor this morning that he wants me to attend."

Yup, Brad was one of those polo-wearing kind of guys. He worked at his father's real estate firm here in the city. They did a lot of commercial investing, from what I gathered at family dinners. I tried not to attend many, but sometimes I had to make an appearance on Brad's arm. His parents worked hard to build the firm and all their investment properties.

When Brad graduated college, he went directly to work at the firm and under his dad. He was making a pretty good salary, but his dad told him he was an employee and needed to work hard if he wanted to become a partner; he wasn't just going to hand a partnership to his son.

Boy, did that piss Brad off?

I think Brad thought he would just walk in and be handed a partnership and a hefty salary, but that didn't happen. He had to work hard and prove himself.

"I'm going to head out and shower at my place; I don't have any suits here," Brad stated.

"Okay, well, I'm going to jump in the shower and try to get some writing done today," I said back to him, getting up from the bed.

"Don't you think you should start letting go of

54

that pipe dream of being the next big songwriter?" Brad said condescendingly as he threw a hoodie on.

"I don't think it's a pipe dream; there are a lot of successful songwriters out there," I shot back.

"Sure, if you say so. Hey, where is your money from last night? I will get that in the bank for you," he said while slipping his arms through a hoodie.

Brad took my tip money every night. He said he put it into a savings account for me so I could save for our future. What a crock of shit. He took that money so he could spend it on extra stuff with his buddies.

God forbid they knew he wasn't making as much money as them. So instead, he took my money. He gave me enough to pay my rent, gas, groceries, and other bills. You would be surprised by how much I made in tips at a dive bar. We were conveniently located close to the colleges, and if a college boy liked what he saw, he tipped you well. Stupid boys!

"I left it on the coffee table; I'm jumping in the shower. If I don't see you when I get out, I will call you later," I said as I exited the bedroom to the bathroom.

Brad didn't say anything; he just started to walk to the living room, so I went into the bathroom and turned on the water to the shower. One great thing about my apartment: it had fantastic water pressure and great hot water. I stepped into the shower and let the heat hit my face. It felt so good to stand there and let the heat of the water hit my body and loosen my tight muscles. After a few minutes of basking in the wonderful hot water, I washed my hair and body.

I shut the water off, and as I opened the hideous fish shower curtain, I jumped when I saw Brad leaning against the vanity. His eyes were extremely dark, almost black. I shivered more from fear than being cold because I was standing there completely naked, with soaking wet hair and no towel. He pushed himself off the vanity, standing straight.

He was not extremely tall; my brothers and Ryan were much taller, but I still had to look up to him. He reached out his arm not to caress me. No, he reached out and grabbed me by the throat and pushed me against the wall beside the shower. My head hit the wall with a hard thump. I could not move with his hand wrapped around my throat, adding just enough pressure to block my airway slightly.

"Brad, please," was all I could get out.

"You think I'm stupid, don't you? You thought I wouldn't catch on to you," he stated in a firm, angry voice. "I don't know what you're talking about. Please let go, and let's talk about this," I continued, "Tell me what has you so upset, Brad, please."

"I saw your fucking phone, and I saw that damn message," again, he had a firm voice.

"What message?"

I tried to think about what could be on my phone, and then it hit me; this was about the texts I sent to Ryan. I was always so careful to delete my texts right after I sent one, especially when it was with Ryan.

Brad hated me having any communication with Ryan. He said it was inappropriate because Ryan would always flirt with me. He really didn't know Ryan thought of me as a sister, no matter how hard I tried growing up to get him to see me as someone more. It's one of the many reasons I left and came here. I was so tired last night I must have forgotten to delete it.

"Why the fuck is Ryan texting you? I told you that shit needed to stop. You disrespectful bitch," Brad seethed.

With one hand still wrapped around my throat and me using both hands trying to get him to let go, he slid his other hand down my stomach and over my pussy.

"How many times have you let him fuck you, you bitch?" Brad yelled.

"No, never," was all I could get out.

"You're fucking lying," he seethed.

"No, I'm not lying," I stated as my eyes began to water.

He seethed again, "You're fucking lying," and before I could react, his hand came back up and smacked me straight across the face.

The sting was overwhelming. Something happened when his hand made contact with my cheek.

I was done. I was done being a victim. I was done with crying. He was not going to get me to beg him to stop. I stared him straight into his eyes, not giving him a reaction to the smack he just gave me. His hand was still wrapped around my throat.

"I'm sick of you lying and disrespecting our relationship," he practically spat in my face with anger.

I said nothing, just kept staring him straight in the eyes. I would not show him any fear.

Again, smack.

I closed my eyes in pain. He got me in the exact same spot. I felt the skin on my right cheek under my eye split open. I felt the blood, but still, I didn't react; I held in the tears and just stared him straight in the eyes again. I knew I was pissing him off more, but I just didn't care. I knew this was not going to end well, but I could not bring myself to beg.

"Get the fuck out of my apartment," I stated firmly. "We're done," I seethed this time.

"Really, we're done? That's what you think?" Brad yelled.

"Yes," I yelled back.

"We're not even close to being done."

Before I could even see what was happening, he punched me and then immediately punched me again. As he let go of my throat, I fell to the floor in excruciating pain.

"Call Jeff and let him know you're not feeling well and that you won't be at work tonight because tonight, you're mine."

Curled up in pain, holding my face, I yelled, "Fuck y—"

Brad kicked me in the stomach, knocking the air from my lungs.

"Call Jeff. You're not going to work tonight. I'll see you later." Brad turned and walked out of the bathroom.

3

MACKENNA

I waited until I heard the apartment door slam shut, then grabbed the top of the vanity and pulled myself up but dropped back down in pain. I hit the tiled floor and just lay there in pain for what felt like hours, but in reality, it was probably only minutes. I started to get cold and realized I was still naked.

Again, I grabbed onto the vanity and pulled myself up successfully this time. I held onto the vanity, peeked up into the mirror, and then gasped at the damage to my face.

My right eye was swelling.

I had a gash on my cheek under my eye. My lip was also starting to swell and had been split open. My stomach was red from where he kicked me. I stared at my reflection in the mirror for some time, trying to figure out what the hell I should do.

If I stayed, Brad would be back. I knew he would come back tonight, probably with flowers and dinner, apologizing for what he would call a misunderstanding.

Fuck him. Not this time.

I left the bathroom and struggled into my bedroom.

Opening my dresser, I grabbed a t-shirt and some leggings and threw them on. Reaching into my closet, I pulled a hoodie off one of the hangers and threw it over my head. Turning to the door, I grabbed my sneakers and went back to the bathroom to try and get a brush through my hair, but seeing myself in the mirror just made me sick. So, I tossed it into a messy bun.

I grabbed my phone. Brad had tossed it at the wall, and it landed on the loveseat.

Thankfully, it was only cracked in a few spots.

The phone made out better than me.

As I slung my crossbody bag over and swiped my keys from the table by the door, I left my apartment. By the time I got to my car, I couldn't even remember if I had locked my door, but I didn't care. I just needed to get out of there.

With shaking hands, I opened a text message to Jeff.

> **Me:** Are you home?

It only took a few seconds for him to reply.

> **Jeff:** Yes, I just woke up.

> **Me:** I need to come over.

> **Jeff:** Okay. Everything okay?

> **Me:** Be there in a few.

I was not about to tell him my fucking asshole boyfriend beat the shit out of me.

It only took about fifteen minutes, and I was knocking on Jeff's door.

My face was swollen, and it hurt so bad. I knew Jeff would be mortified the moment he opened the door.

I stood there with my head down, trying to cover my face and the tears that were falling down my cheek.

Jeff opened the door and, without saying a word, wrapped his arms around me and squeezed gently. That was all it took, and I just broke.

The squealing cries came out of me. Jeff had to hold me up and lead me into his apartment. Jeff's apartment was not much, but it was bigger than mine.

He guided me into his living room, which was past the kitchen like my layout. His living room was much larger and had a slider door that went to a small balcony. I sat on the brown leather sofa, and Jeff wrapped a grey throw blanket around my shoulders.

I didn't realize I was shivering until he wrapped the blanket around me.

Jeff sat beside me, wrapping his arms around me to help me from shaking.

"Kenna, what the hell happened? I think we need to get you to the hospital," Jeff said with concern in his voice.

"No, no, just give me a few minutes," I cried.

We sat in silence until the tears stopped, and I could catch my breath. Jeff was slowly rubbing my back to help me calm down.

"Let me get you some ice for the swelling," Jeff finally spoke after being silent for so long. He got up from the sofa to walk over to the kitchen. I could hear him shuffling around to get a dish towel and the smacking ice hitting the counter from the ice tray. A moment later, Jeff took the seat beside me again and slowly started to place the ice on my face. I flinched from the pain.

"I'm sorry," Jeff whispered.

I grabbed the ice pack from his hands. I tried to

smile, but it was just too painful. My head was pounding not only from the pain but from the crying.

"Can I have a glass of water?" I asked Jeff. My mouth was so dry.

"Yeah, sure, hold on. I will grab it for you," Jeff said as he walked back to the fridge. He continued speaking, "Can you please tell me what happened?"

I knew there was nothing I could do but tell him everything. Jeff knew Brad was not the greatest guy. He knew Brad was jealous, possessive, and controlling. Jeff would see Brad at the bar sometimes when we worked.

There were times a customer would flirt with me, and because I was working mostly for tips, I flirted back. I tried to explain to Brad all the time that it was just part of the job, and it never actually meant anything. Brad never believed me. He would just grab my arm and pull me closer and whisper in my ear, usually to tell me that I was a slut or a piece of shit.

I knew Jeff saw it, and sometimes he could even hear Brad utter the disgusting comments. But Jeff never saw Brad hit me, nor did I ever tell him that Brad had beaten me.

There were a few times I had a black eye or bruised arm, but I became pretty good at coming up with an excuse about how clumsy I was. There was the time I told him I tripped over my guitar and smacked my face against the wall or the time I told him I slipped in the shower.

When Jeff came back into the room and handed me the glass of water, he asked again for me to tell him what had happened. I took a long sip of water and decided to just tell him.

"Brad hit me," was all I could say.

"Fuck that. He did more than hit you; he beat the shit out of you. Look at you."

"Please, Jeff," I begged.

"No, enough with the lies. I want to know the truth. I sat around watching you show up to work with bruises and you asking me to hide money for you for almost a year. I deserve to know the truth," Jeff said with anger coursing in his voice.

And he did. He deserved to know it all. He was right. I had been asking him to hold a portion of my tips without giving him any reason why, and because Jeff was such a great guy, he did it with no questions asked.

"Tell me, Kenna, please," he pleaded.

"I got out of the shower," I started, with new tears stinging my eyes. "Brad was there," I said.

As I replayed what happened, Jeff's face turned to sympathy for me, and then as I continued with everything, his face turned to anger. He got up from the sofa and started to pace, and then I heard the crash. Jeff had taken the table lamp and thrown it against the wall. I jumped, and Jeff immediately ran over to me.

"Kenna, I'm so sorry. I didn't mean to scare you. I just—fuck, I don't even know what to say or do right now. This is fucking crazy. I knew he was hurting you; I knew you were feeding me a bunch of bullshit. You are not going back to him. Please tell me you are not going back to him," Jeff pleaded.

"No, I'm done. If I don't, it will just keep getting worse. God, I don't even know how I could let it get this bad. When we met, he was so sweet, caring, and affectionate. I can't even tell you when it started to change," I cried.

My mind drifted to how I met Brad. I was writing songs in college for local musicians in the city. I actually got a pretty good name locally. I had bands reaching out to me for help with songs.

Sometimes I would write the songs, and sometimes they just wanted help with a song they were writing. There were times I performed duets with some of the local bands, and I even performed with them at some of the college bars around the city. I even performed in the shithole I worked at on numerous occasions.

One local band and I wrote a few songs together that were duets. They had been hired to perform at a wedding at a fancy country club right outside the city. I think the guitarist was the brother of the bride. I remember at a few of the gigs.

Brad was good friends with the groom. I remember Brad coming up to me at the end of the night when I was packing up my things. He had a flower from one of the centerpieces. He told me my voice was amazing.

We talked for a few minutes, and he asked for my number. I thought he was cute, so what the hell? I gave him my number, and a week later, we went out on our first date.

Jeff dragged me out of my thoughts, "Kenna, I think we should go to the cops and file a report and hopefully get a restraining order. I can't imagine you getting denied one."

I lifted my eyes up at Jeff. I know the statistics I knew a restraining order was just a piece of paper, and I also knew Brad's parents would do what was needed to keep their son from getting arrested or having charges filed against him.

"No, I need to leave."

"What do you mean leave?" Jeff asked.

"Jeff, I need to leave Massachusetts. I need to go home," I said, tongue and cheek.

"Home, you are going to go home? To Florida?"

"Yes."

"Shit," Jeff whispered, looking down and then back up into my tear-filled eyes. "When?"

"Now," is all I said. I didn't need to say anymore Jeff knew it was now or never.

Over the past few months, Brad has been getting angrier and angrier. He assumed he would be a partner in his Daddy's firm, and the more time that went on where he was not, the angrier he got. That anger was being directed at me.

Today in the bathroom was not the first time Brad held me by the throat. Two weeks ago, we went to dinner with his parents and some associates.

His father spent most of the dinner singing the praises of one of the associates who had just closed a multimillion-dollar deal. I could see Brad fidgeting at the table, ordering more drinks than usual. That was the first time I had to drive his BMW. That was a graduation present from his parents. Brad was drunk, and I knew it was not going to be a good end to the night. I had tried to drop him at his place, but he insisted on coming to my apartment.

Once we got up to my apartment, he got rough. He tore my shirt to get to my breast. I pushed him back and told him he was drunk and it was late. Brad latched on to my throat and pushed me against the wall. That was the first time I truly feared for my life.

He took two steps to close the gap between us, leaned down to my ear, and whispered, "You are such a fucking tease. I'm going to bed." And then, he bit my earlobe hard.

When he let me go and walked to my bedroom, I dropped to the floor and stayed there the rest of the night.

"What about your lease and all your stuff?' I heard Jeff ask while he put his hand on my shoulder to bring me back from the horrible memory I was having.

"Brad is at work, so I will go back and grab my clothes, my guitar, and a few personal items, but the rest I don't care about. The landlord can toss it. When I'm on the road, I will email the landlord and explain the situation and hope he lets me out of my lease. If not fuck it, I don't care I need to go now. Brad will come back tonight I can't go through this again. I can't." I ended the comment with a deep breath.

Jeff walked down the hall to his bedroom and returned, handing me the debit card. Not long after working at the bar Jeff and I went to lunch after I asked him if we could stop at the bank that was across the street. We went in, and he waited as I opened an account. As we were leaving the bank and Jeff walked me to my car, I handed him a debit card.

Looking down, Jeff asked, "What's this?"

"It's a debit card, dummy," I chuckled.

"I know it's a debit card, but why are you giving it to me?" he asked.

"I know we don't know each other that well, but I trust you. Can you please hold onto this for me?"

"Are you doing something illegal?" he asked, lifting one brow.

"God, no! Nothing like that." I held my stomach, laughing. "I just have a habit of losing things," I lied. That was the first of many lies I would end up telling Jeff.

That night, when we finished work, I handed him a portion of my tips and asked if he would deposit it into the account, also giving him a stack of deposit slips. Jeff eyed me cautiously, trying to figure out why I would ask him to take my money and trust him to deposit it. But Jeff, being the sweetheart he is, just took it and said, "Sure, I'll make the deposit for you."

That was the kind of friend Jeff was—no, is—he would do anything for you. That's why I never told him everything; I knew he would react and he would get hurt. Jeff was a solid guy, but he was no fighter; he was a writer. It was more than that, though. I didn't want him to look at me the way he did when I arrived at his apartment. I was ashamed of my situation.

How could someone like me end up in an abusive relationship? I grew up with tough brothers who taught me to take care of myself in a dangerous situation. Somehow, I cowered down and became weak, or at least that's what I thought of myself.

Looking at the debit card, I slipped it into the side pocket of my leggings. I then reached up around Jeff's neck and pulled him into a hug. I squeezed even though it hurt. I had to say goodbye to my best friend I made here. More than that, I was saying goodbye to a person who became family here, the only family I had here. Tears started to roll down my cheek onto Jeff's shirt.

"Don't cry," he said, possibly feeling his shirt getting wet. "You leave here and don't look back. I'll take care of whatever you need done here. This isn't goodbye; I promise I'll see you again. I can come visit you in Florida."

"You promise you'll stay in touch with me and come see me?"

"Palm trees and warm weather—of course, I'll come see you," Jeff said with a calming smile that almost showed that cute dimple he had.

That was Jeff, always making me smile even

when I was at my worst. "I'll miss you so much," I whispered to him.

"Let me come help you pack up, please."

"No, it's okay. I can do it. If you return with me, it will be too hard to leave."

"I'll miss you so much."

"And I'll miss you. Thank you, Jeff, for every-thing." I lifted my face up to meet Jeff's eyes and pulled him down to kiss his cheek. "I'll text you when I get on the road." And with one last hug, I slipped out of his embrace, then out the door running to my car.

4

MACKENNA

It was still early in the morning, only ten o'clock, and I knew Brad would be coming back in the evening. So, I had some time to get all my stuff together, but I was not about to waste any time. I wanted to be out of the state before he showed up to find me here. I ran around my apartment, gathering anything that was important to me.

I got my guitar in its case and gathered my writing journals that were lingering around the apartment. I had journals located in several places because I never wanted to have to find one when something came to my mind. I wanted to have it written down as soon as it hit me. I took the small plastic bin under my bathroom vanity and gathered up all my toiletries, and threw the lid on top.

When I went to leave the bathroom, I caught

myself in the mirror and could see the bruises begin-
ning to come out. I didn't move for a good minute,
just staring at myself in the mirror, hating myself for
letting a man do this to me.

Anger and hate were brewing in me, and I lifted
my arm and slammed the mirror with my fist.

"Fuck," I yelled. "Get yourself together, Kenna.
You need to hurry up," I said to myself.

I quickly went into my bedroom and yanked the
small suitcase I had stored under my bed. I grabbed
all my panties and bras, as well as many clothes as I
could fit into the suitcase. I loaded another bag with
shoes and anything else I could from my closet.
After taking my phone charger that was plugged into
the wall, I made my way back to the front of my
apartment with my suitcase in my hand—not the
one I hit the mirror with. That one was a little cut up
from the glass—and the bag draped on my shoulder.
I looked around and realized I had just packed up
my life in less than an hour.

"Shit, I truly had nothing here," I thought.

It only took two quick trips to get my car loaded.
I took one last look up at my apartment on the
second floor and, with a deep breath, turned back to
my car and got in.

As I pulled out of the parking lot, I wiped away
the tears that came out of my burning eyes.

I had a thirteen-hundred-mile drive to get from hell to home. I had nothing planned out, just all my stuff loaded in my blue Toyota Camry, the same car that brought me to Massachusetts. That drive seemed like a lifetime ago, but in reality, it was just over four years ago. So much had happened in those years. I had come to Massachusetts for school and to follow my dreams of becoming a songwriter and, on my own two feet, away from my overprotective father and brothers.

Don't get me wrong, I loved each one of them, but I was never going to find myself under their wings. I needed to become independent. I needed to learn who I was and who I could become. I never guessed in those few years. I would find myself running from a man who hurt me emotionally, mentally, and physically.

I had my foot on the gas and was headed down I-95 toward New York City. I had enough gas to get to Connecticut before I would need to stop. Focusing on the road ahead of me, I could feel my palms starting to sweat from gripping the steering wheel so hard. My mind was going into a tunnel of memories.

I was so happy and excited to start my adventure in college. I arrived motivated and determined to make my dreams a reality. Everything started perfectly. I was writing all the time, writing about happiness, adventure, and independence. It didn't take long to find myself at open mic nights singing my songs. That's how I met so many local artists. I somehow found myself writing songs for other bands, which is what I liked. I had a good voice and grew up singing. My mother was a singer, and she taught me to play the guitar.

My mind started to go back to when I was little, probably around eight years old, when my mother bought me my first guitar and sat with me daily, teaching me how to play. When I was ten, I wrote my first song. It was about a butterfly and a flower. It wasn't any good, but my mother learned the song and helped me put it on the guitar and would sing it with me.

Taking flight like a butterfly, searching for the brightness in life.

This verse always brought a smile to both of our faces. My mother was beautiful with long red hair. It was wavy like mine but fell all the way down her back. Her eyes were green, almost an emerald color. I looked a lot like my mother; we both had red hair and green eyes, but my eyes never sparked the emerald color she had. She would look at me with such pride and love. It always made me wish I had her bright shade of emerald eyes.

One day, her emerald eyes just didn't shine as

brightly. She became tired all the time. I would come home from school, and she would be napping. I was young but knew something was going on. She was getting fragile and became very weak. I can remember the last time I was with her. She had gotten so weak that nurses were starting to come into our home. I would lay in bed with her and hold her hand, the hand that held mine, strumming the cords of the guitar she had taught me to play, had turned thin and fragile as if I would crush her hand with the slightest grip.

"Let your voice be heard, my beautiful girl. You have so much to give this world with your voice. I will always be listening to the beautiful melodies that come from my butterfly." Those were the last words my mother spoke to me.

It was a Tuesday evening in February when my mother passed away from ovarian cancer. I was in my room playing my guitar when I could hear my brothers crying and my daddy telling them it would be okay. I could not bring myself to leave my room. I just sat on my bed with the guitar that my mother gifted me and played until my fingers started to hurt, and my eyes grew too tired from what felt like endless tears.

I was so deep into my thoughts of my mother that I hadn't realized I was hitting the border of

Connecticut. I peeked at my gas tank and knew I would need to stop at the next stop to get gas. As I pulled up to the gas pump, I grabbed my sunglasses from the passenger seat in hopes of hiding the bruising and black eye that was starting to really show.

While I pumped my gas, I scanned around at all the people in the rest area either getting gas or coming in and out of the store with snacks for the road. I saw a mother holding her daughter's hand tight as they left the store and walked back to their car. I began to hum the very first song I wrote, butterflies and flowers, and I could see the memory clear as day in my mind of my mother and me sitting in the backyard, her emerald eyes beaming at me as we sang the song together.

It had been over a decade since my mother was gone, but in moments like right now, I could feel her like she was right beside me, whispering in my ear, *'Let your voice be heard.'*

I needed to get my voice back.

5

MACKENNA

Heading back onto I-95, the sun was shining bright. I still had a couple more hours before the sun would set and Brad would return to my vacant apartment. I changed my phone to silent because I knew the moment he saw my stuff gone, he would freak out and blow up my phone with calls and texts. I didn't want to hear it. I just wanted to keep going and get as far away as I possibly could. For the first time in a long time, I wanted to be home.

The big question was, what would home be like now? It had been over a year since I'd been back home. The last time I was there was for my daddy's funeral. My big tough dad was very overprotective of me and instilled that family-first mentality on my brothers.

He would always say, "Boys, she is your number

one. You'll always make sure she is taken care of and protected."

One time, when I was twelve, there was a boy in my class giving me a hard time. Everyone thought he had a crush on me. I don't remember his name. He moved away right before high school, but at the time, he lived in our neighborhood. One day, he was riding his bike by my house with a few of his friends, and he yelled something mean to me. To be honest, I was too busy playing my guitar on the front porch to even notice what he yelled, but my daddy heard him as he was working on the car in the driveway.

That night at dinner, he told me never to let a boy talk to me that way and that I would need to start going to the gym a few times a week to learn some moves to protect myself. I chuckled to myself, thinking, what good that did. I wanted no part in the gym, but I never said no to Daddy, so I smiled and said, "Okay."

He looked at both my brothers and said, "What is your sister?" Conor, without missing a beat, said, "Our number one."

My daddy smiled and said, "That's right. Now I expect you to take care of that boy. He is never to bother Mackenna again. Got it?"

"I'm on it, Dad," Conor and Finn both said in unison.

A couple of days later, that boy had a black eye and limped for a week. It was me. I had made my way to my daddy's gym and tried to learn a few fighting moves to please my dad. I was never any good at it and only went for about a year before Daddy let me stop going. Ryan and my bothers, on the other hand, were not happy that I stopped going.

As the sun started to set and I had to put my headlights on, I brought myself back to the now. I left Massachusetts with no plan, and now I was getting tired. When I left, I was running on adrenaline. Now, my body was getting tired and starting to ache, not to mention my face hurt something fierce. I was just hitting Delaware, and it was only six-thirty in the evening. I should probably get a few more hours in, maybe stop someplace in Virginia.

I knew it would be hard because of the pain I was in, but I was determined to keep going. That determination paid off, and a couple of hours later, I was in Virginia.

There were a few hotels at the next exit, so I decided it was time to get off and get a room at one of the hotels. The lady working at the front desk of the hotel that I pulled into was looking at me with sadness in her eyes. I knew that sadness and sympathy were for me. I didn't check the mirror in my car, but by the way my face felt, I knew it was worse than it was earlier.

After taking the elevator to the third floor, my room was five doors down the hall. I entered a room that had two double beds and a nightstand between the two. The room was no five-star hotel, but it was clean, and I just needed a bed to sleep in. I pulled the covers back and slowly slipped into the bed, not even changing my clothes. As I closed my eyes, I thought about home and drifted off to sleep.

I opened my eyes to darkness. I didn't even remember falling asleep, but it was still dark, so I sat up a little, looking at the bedside clock. It took a minute for my eyes to adjust, and I saw it was only four in the morning. Laying there, I started calculating how long of a drive it would be and if I could do it in one day by myself with as much pain as I was in. The room was quiet and dark, and I just lay there with my thoughts.

What will my brothers do when they see me? How will I tell them I was in an abusive relationship? I was not afraid of my brothers; I was more afraid of them jumping on a flight and then ending up in prison for murder. I was their number one, after all. Our Daddy instilled that in their brains.

Slowly, I dragged myself out of the bed and over to the bathroom. Turning the shower on and removing my clothes. My body ached so much I needed to get under the hot water in hopes it would loosen my body. I avoided the mirror over the sink and opened the glass shower doors. I stood under the shower until the water turned cold. I was awake now, and there was no sense in sitting around a hotel, so I threw on the same clothes because I was too tired to take anything out of my car last night.

As I made my way out of the bathroom and back to the bed, I grabbed my phone out of my bag and sat on the bed. I knew I would regret looking, but I could not help myself. There it was: twenty-one missed calls, and I don't even know how many texts from Brad. I skipped those and went to the text from Jeff.

Jeff 07:00 pm: When you stop driving, can you please let me know you're okay, all right?

Jeff 08:30 pm: Are you still driving?

Jeff 10:00 pm: Oh, shit. Brad was just here looking for you.

Jeff 10:00 pm: It was not good.

> Jeff 10:00 pm: Chris had to drag him out of the bar.

Chris was the bouncer who worked Friday and Saturday nights at the bar. He was a full-time security guard at one of the colleges and worked for extra money at the bar dealing with more college kids.

> Me: Sorry, once I got to the hotel, I fell right to sleep, never looking at my phone.

> Me: I'm in VA now.

> Me: But I'm going to head back on the road.

> Me: Please be careful of Brad.

> Me: I'm sorry I got you messed up in this.

I knew there was no way Jeff was up to answer, so I slipped the phone back into my bag after quickly deleting the texts from Brad before I could read them.

I was done with that asshole.

6

MACKENNA

After checking out and grabbing a large coffee from the breakfast area of the hotel, I was on the road again. This would be a long day with a twelve-hour drive left, but I was determined to get there.

"Ugh, what's that smell?" I opened the car window to let some air in. "Oh, that's me!"

I probably should have brought in a change of clothes, but whatever, it didn't matter as long as I could get home. I had to chuckle as I thought back to the last time I went without a change of clothes. My mind went back to when I was . . . I think, thirteen. My daddy had to go to a fight that one of his *Trod Aire's* were in.

Trod Aire means fighter in Irish and what my daddy would call anyone he trained. He was in Miami, I think, for that fight. I was going to stay at my friend Chrissy's house, and my brothers and Ryan were going camping.

That morning Chrissy called me to let me know she got grounded for sneaking out, which meant I was going camping with my brothers. To say they were pissed would be an understatement. At thirteen, I didn't know what to pack, nor did my brothers think to pack for me. I swear they had a bet going for who could scare me the most. Each one of them told me a scary story and then stuck me in a tent to sleep. I think that was the first time I ever stayed up all night. Ryan was the only one who checked on me that night.

"You okay in there?" he had called into my tent.

"No, you guys are assholes," I whispered because who knows who was in the woods watching and waiting to murder us, or so at least I thought in my young, naïve mind.

I shook my head, trying to get myself focused on the road. I really needed to stop thinking about the past and focus on the now and getting back home. I decided I needed music, reaching down I plugged my phone into the auxiliary cord.

Yup, I had a cord to hook my phone to my car. No Bluetooth in this car.

I swiped my phone and went to one of my playlists. As The Lumineers came through the speakers and they sang about driving through the state and through the night, I focused on I-95 and doing the same. The next few hours, I stayed focused and determined, and before I knew it, I was hitting the border of South Carolina. At that point, I was drained and needed to stop for a break.

It only took a few minutes until I approached the next rest stop. I pulled in and got out of the car, stretched, and headed to the bathroom. As I washed my hands, the woman next to me stared over with concern on her face.

"Are you okay?" she asked. "I can help you. My husband is right outside. We can help you."

I glanced at her for a moment and then realized she was concerned because of what my face looked like.

"Oh no, thank you. I'm okay," I said to the woman in the bathroom. I could tell she was genuinely concerned for me, but I didn't want to involve anyone else. "I'm heading home to my family now."

The nice woman smiled and nodded before turning to leave. As she peeked over her shoulder, she said, "You are so brave. You keep going, and don't you look back."

I eyed myself in the dirty mirror that was lined on the wall and thought about how I had ended up bruised and battered. I was determined not to shed one more tear and to keep moving.

By the time I hit Georgia, I started to wonder what I was going to do when I got to Orlando. I knew I would be exhausted by the time I made it, and I didn't want to have to deal with my brothers' reaction. They had no idea I was coming, let alone that I was in an abusive relationship. Just thinking about the words "abusive relationship" made me sick.

At that moment, I realized I couldn't just pull up to the house I grew up in and walk in as if nothing had happened. I hurt, and I was exhausted. I spent the whole drive through Georgia trying to figure out what I would do. It wasn't until I hit Jacksonville, Florida, that I thought of Chrissy.

With "Coming Home" by Skylar Grey playing through the car speakers, I thought about Chrissy, my very best friend, since we were in diapers. Both our moms were best friends, and they lived around the corner from us.

As I smiled at the memory, I reached for my phone and noticed about a hundred texts from Brad. I carefully swiped the phone and pulled up Chrissy's number. It was only one ring before she picked it up.

"Holy shit, Kenna, is that you?" Chrissy yelled out.

"Hey, Chrissy. It's me."

"OMG, it's so good to hear your voice. I miss you so much," Chrissy practically yelled through the phone with excitement.

I left Florida and had gone away to college. Chrissy stayed back and went to Florida State. She graduated a year ago with a marketing degree. We constantly stayed in contact through texts and social media, but like everyone else, she wasn't aware of the situation I'd been living in.

"Guess what? I just got back to Florida. I'm just passing the Daytona exit, and I was wondering if I could come to see you. Is that okay?" I asked.

"Are you fucking kidding me? Of course. Holy shit, I can't believe you are here! Conor didn't tell me you were coming to town." Well, that was a surprise. I was not aware that she and Conor spoke that much.

"Conor doesn't know, and neither does Finn. It was a spur-of-the-moment trip," I said through the phone that was being held between my shoulder and injured cheek.

Before I could finish my sentence, Chrissy eagerly responded, "Yes, come here. I can't wait to see you. I moved a few months ago. I will text you my address now."

"Thanks, Chris. I should be there in a little over an hour."

As I ended the call, the text was already coming through with Chrissy's address.

Waking up the next morning with the smell of coffee brewing in the air, I felt at ease for the first time in a long time. When I arrived at Chrissy's place last night, she was mortified by what she saw. She held her hand to my cheek, and for the first time in days, I allowed myself to truly break down. I grabbed her and hugged her with my head on her shoulder.

I cried so hard my body shook, and my legs gave out. I pulled Chrissy to the floor as I went down. I could not stop it. The weight of everything just took over me. Chrissy didn't fight it. She just lowered her body with mine and continued to hold me in the middle of her apartment hallway. I'm not sure how long we were out there, but at some point, she pulled me up to my feet and brought me into her apartment and down the hall to her bed.

"Shhh, Kenna, just go to sleep. We will talk in the morning. I'm right here, and I'm not going anywhere," she whispered.

Blinking my eyes to adjust to the Florida sun entering her bedroom window, I noticed Chrissy leaning against the door jamb with two cups of coffee in her hands. "I got you some coffee. You still take it with just cream?" she asked.

"Yes," I said, wiping my eyes.

"Here you go." She handed me a pink coffee cup.

Slowly, I pushed myself up into a sitting position. I must have moaned with pain because Chrissy immediately asked, "Are you okay?"

"I am . . . or, at least, I will be."

"Are you going to tell me what happened?"

With tears fighting to come out, I started telling Chrissy everything. I purged everything, and Chrissy just sat there with her free hand holding mine. After about an hour of narrating my shitty life for the past year, Chrissy lifted my hand, kissed it, and climbed back into the bed with me, sitting with me in silence. No lecture, no judgment, just my best friend being present with me.

I knew the question would come, so I was not surprised when Chrissy finally spoke an hour later. "Shit, Kenna, what are you going to tell Conor and Finn?"

Dread was now looming over me because, truthfully, I was incredibly nervous to tell my brothers anything. "Shit," was all I could manage to utter at that moment.

By the time we finally got out of bed, it was

nearly noon. I helped Chrissy make the bed. "Ryan is going to fucking freak out," Chrissy softly said.

"What do you mean?" I lifted the pretty pale green comforter up and threw the pillows with pink and yellow flowers onto the bed.

"Oh, come on, Kenna, please don't tell me you don't think Ryan is going to lose his mind when he finds out someone did that to you." She pointed at my bruised and swollen face.

"No, I'm sure he'll be upset. He is family, like a brother." I stared back at her.

"Yeah, okay, Kenna, if you say so."

Chrissy always thought Ryan thought more of me. She thinks Ryan had feelings for me, but that was just crazy. Ryan is best friends with my brothers, and he was always there giving me just as much shit as my brothers whenever I tagged along and annoyed them.

I shook off the comment from Chrissy and moved my way out of the bedroom into . . .

Wow! I didn't get to notice how beautiful her apartment was last night.

The apartment was probably twice the size of mine in Boston. It had high ceilings with exposed duct work. One of the living room walls was exposed brick, and there was a large beige sofa against it. On the adjacent wall, there were large

French Doors that led to, from what I could see, a very large terrace. The television on the other wall was huge. It had to be sixty-five inches.

Chrissy always loved curling up and watching movies. The unit was an open floor plan that had a massive white marble island dividing the kitchen and the living space. The kitchen almost blew me away. It had grey cabinets lining the back wall with top-of-the-line stainless steel appliances. Apparently, marketing was paying off for Chrissy. Chrissy nearly walked right into me because of the way I stopped at her bedroom door, taking in the beautiful apartment.

Breathless from surprise, I stated, "This place is absolutely amazing."

"Thanks, Kenna. It has a second bedroom across the way." She pointed to the door across the room. "You can stay as long as you want."

7

MACKENNA

After taking a long shower and grabbing my belongings from the car, I indulged in two more cups of coffee before making my way out of Chrissy's apartment. She headed off to work while I headed to the one place I dreaded the most—Mickey's Gym.

As much as I wanted to hide in Chrissy's beautiful apartment until the bruises healed, I knew there was no way they wouldn't find out I was here. Chrissy was my best friend, but I knew she would be unable to lie to Conor if she saw him. Chrissy and Conor always had a bizarre friendship.

My dad had turned this gym into a gem of downtown Orlando. Fighters came from all around the world to train at this gym. As I pulled into the parking lot, I was blown away by the new appearance. I hadn't been here in years, not even when I came back for my daddy's funeral. I couldn't bring myself to come here.

As I stepped out of the car, I cringed at the sign that was above the building - Micky's Gym. Micky is what my daddy always called me. Only my daddy and my brothers called me that. My daddy said having a daughter was the first time he knew he would do anything to protect me, that he would fight to the end to protect me. Something he wanted his fighters to have. He had the passion and strength to fight to the end, so he named his gym after his only daughter. I smiled at the thought and then dropped my chin, wondering what my daddy would do if he was here now.

My daddy fought and saved to buy this small building that was once a car dealership. It was closed and abandoned long before he bought it. He got it cheap and restored the structure and windows. He gutted the inside and covered the floors with mats, there was a room for weightlifting, another room with bikes and treadmills for cardio, and then there was a room that had an octagon in the center of it.

As I walked into the gym that I had watched my daddy build, I smiled at the cute girl working the front desk. She looked up at me. "You are Micky, aren't you?"

"I am, but no one calls me that but my daddy and brothers."

"Yes, of course, I'm sorry. It's Mackenna, correct?"

"You can call me that or Kenna. Are my brothers here?"

"They are. Last I checked, they were meeting in Conor's office."

"I'm going to head back, thanks!"

When I turned to walk away, I could feel her eyes on me, probably wondering what could have happened to me. I kept walking, never looking back. I walked through each room, trying not to be noticed. I knew a lot of these fighters and didn't want to be stopped. I needed to see my brothers first. In all honesty, my heart was beating out of my chest in fear that one particular fighter would see me. I didn't know what I would do if I saw his face, especially right now.

I made it to the back of the gym unnoticed and knocked on Conor's office door, slowly opening it. Finn turned from the seat he was in across from my brother, and Conor lifted his head. I could see the shock on both their faces.

My brothers were big and strong, and I watched both their faces change from shock to anger immediately. Finn jumped from his seat and only needed to take one big step over to me. I couldn't stop myself. I jumped into my brothers' arms and hugged him so tight, hoping he would not let me go.

Conor didn't move from the desk. As I looked up around my brother's shoulder, I could see Conor gripping his desk, his knuckles turning white, and his jaw tight.

"Who the fuck did this to you?" Conor roared.

I slowly slipped out of Finn's embrace and faced Conor. Tears were trickling out of my eyes; I could feel blood on my cheek from my wound opening from the tight hold Finn had on me. Finn lowered himself to my level and gripped my chin to look at me.

"Kenna, what happened to you?" Finn asked in what felt like a whisper compared to Conor's roar.

I looked directly at Finn and let the tears release from my eyes. Finn wrapped his arms around me once more and whispered words that I could not make out but I'm sure were explicit. He dragged me over to a leather loveseat that, even in my current state, I knew was not here the last time I was. I leaned into Finn as he guided us to sit, but before my ass hit the cushion, I jumped from the massive bang and then another one by the third bang, I knew it was Conor shoving his fists hard into his desk.

"Who the fuck did this to you," Conor roared again.

"Stop, Conor, just fucking stop. You are scaring her," Finn stated firmly.

Conor slowly came around his desk and knelt down in front of me. He gently put his hands on my knees, which I could feel were shaking. "Kenna, look at me, please—please, tell me who did this to you, so I can fucking kill them."

"Brad," is all I whispered and looked down in shame. Shame for what I don't know. I knew this was not my fault, but I still felt shame.

Finn, my massively calm brother, continued to hold me as Conor lost complete control. I could not make out the words he said over the banging of his fists against the wall. I managed to pull myself out of Finn's arms and jump to my feet, hitting Conor hard in the back and begging him to stop.

"Stop, fucking stop, Conor, enough," I roared this time. "Please, enough. I can't take anymore," I said in a somewhat lower voice.

Conor dropped his forehead against the wall and whispered what I thought was, "I'm supposed to protect you."

"We're not doing this right now. I came home. I'm home . . . I left Brad, I left, and now I'm home. That's it. Brad isn't here he can't hurt me again," I said in a broken voice.

I could see Finn understand I was not rehashing what happened, especially with them. I was here to move on, to move on where I felt the safest with them. After a few more minutes of silence and consoling hugs, Conor stated in a firm, deep voice with dark, angry eyes, not at me but at the failure he felt for not protecting me. "When did you get here?"

"I got here last night. I stayed with Chrissy."

"Chrissy? You got here last fucking night, and she didn't tell me?" Conor stated in disbelief.

"She knew I needed to be the one to tell you."

Conor shook his head in disbelief or anger who knows? "We can go get your stuff and bring it to the house."

"No," I yelled, "Chrissy is letting me stay with her, and I want to stay with her."

"For fuck's sake, Kenna, you—" Conor started.

Finn jumped in, "Let's have dinner tonight, and we can discuss everything. This is not the place for us to be discussing this."

That's when I peeked over and noticed the blinds open to the windows that lead out to the gym with frozen fighters staring in.

I headed for the door, then looking over my shoulder, I said, "I will be over around six."

I didn't wait for a response. I just opened the door and walked out of my brother's office and out of the gym.

8

RYAN

With Beastie Boys jamming through my AirPods and adding weight to the barbell, I peeked up, my dick twitching immediately. I knew that body, that gorgeous hourglass figure. I secretly stared at that body as a teenager—the long red wavy hair that I imagined wrapped around my hands.

Kenna is here. What was she doing here, and when did she get here?

I stopped everything and followed her. I watched her walk out of the gym and to that same blue Camry, I saw her leave in five years ago. She never turned around. I only got to see the back of her perfect silhouette, but I couldn't complain. I enjoyed the back view just as much as the front.

Once she pulled out of the parking lot, I ran, not walked to Conor's office.

"Holy shit, Kenna is here," I yelled as I entered Conor's office.

"She just got back," Finn stated. He looked pissed when he should look happy to see his sister.

"What's going on?" I asked.

"Motherfucker hit her," Conor literally spit the words out.

"Wait, what? Who hit who?" I asked, looking between both Finn and Conor.

Conor would not answer, so Finn said, "Kenna."

My hands balled into fists.

"What the fuck do you mean, Finn? What about Kenna?" I roared.

"She is coming to dinner tonight," is all he said, looking down at my hands curled into a tight fists, making my knuckles white.

Conor was naive to my feelings toward Kenna, but Finn knew how I felt about her. At least he knew when we were in high school. He caught me many times checking his sister out. We never spoke of it because I would never act on my feelings. I don't know if it was exactly a feeling more like I wanted her sweet pussy wrapped around my cock.

Finn knew there was no way I had a death wish because Conor would murder me if I made a move on his little sister. So, I bottled up all those feelings and pretended I only saw Conor and Finn's little sister as my own little sister.

"I will fucking be there," I stated, looking Finn directly in the eyes, eyes I knew were showing just as much anger as his and Conor's.

I walked out before Conor could even jump in because I was not sure if he saw me acting as a protective older brother or a man who wanted nothing more than to protect and claim her.

There was no way I was going to weight train. I needed to smash my fists into something or someone.

"Jax," I yelled to the newbie, "Get your fucking ass on the mat, now!"

After about an hour of sparring, I exited the octagon to the locker room to grab my bag. I would shower at home. I needed to get the fuck out of here and figure out what happened to Kenna. I tried to think where she would be. I know she isn't at her brother's house because they said she was coming over for dinner, so that meant she was either at a hotel or staying with someone.

"Fuck," I yelled through the car.

Dropping my head to the steering wheel, feeling like I failed another important woman in my life. With my head resting on the steering wheel of my brand-new F-150 truck that I gifted myself for my last win, my thoughts drifted to memories I stuffed so deep inside myself years ago. Now years later, here I am, faced again with a woman who means everything to me, hurt and battered.

Kenna, my Kenna is hurt.

With rage boiling in me, I stepped on the brake and pushed the button to start my truck. Roaring out of the parking lot, barely looking to see if any cars were coming, I sped down the main road, taking several left and right turns until I was there facing my past, the past I buried. I had not been here in what felt like a lifetime ago.

Parked in the visitor's lot, I stared down the little beaten-up road at the mobile home I grew up in. It was still as small as I remembered, if not smaller. I was sure that a new family lives there now, and I wondered if they knew what horrible things happened there. I gripped the steering wheel hard as I thought about a frail woman, beaten and bloody. I could not tell where the blood was coming from. I can still see myself holding her when I was so small, trying to comfort her and take her pain away.

"Mom, shh, it's okay," I would whisper to not disturb the monster who had retreated to the back bedroom.

"Ryan, baby, go, go now, stay at Conor and

Finn's," my mother spoke with blood coming from her mouth.

There was no way I was leaving her. He could come out at any time and attack her again. She was my mother. I would protect her. I always heard Conor and Finn's Daddy tell them, "you protect the women, that's what a man does." I would be a man; I will protect my mother. That night, like many other nights, I had her sleep in my bed as I laid on the floor guarding her with my life.

Shaking my head, I removed my hands from the wheel and rubbed them across my face, hoping that would make the memory go away. It didn't work. The memories started to flood my mind. I could see it like it was yesterday: the ambulance, the police all in front of my home, the monster who lived there being dragged out.

I ran to it, yelling, "Mom. Mom. Mom."

A cop tried to stop me, but I was bigger. I was a teenage boy who worked out and trained. That monster waited for me to not be home, and then he attacked.

As I stared at my hands, I could still see the blood on them from dropping to my mother's motionless body that laid in the shitty kitchen that was in the middle of the mobile home. With my heart racing so fast, I thought for sure it would beat right out of my chest.

I leaned my face down to hers and kissed her forehead, stroking her blood-soaked hair, crying, "Momma, I'm so sorry. I'm so very sorry. Please don't leave me. I'm sorry I wasn't here to protect you, but I will never let it happen again, I promise."

That promise didn't matter. She was gone. My mother was beaten to death, and I was not there to keep her safe.

What kind of son am I?

That night changed everything. I left that mobile home park, never to return until right now when I failed another woman. A woman who was just a girl when I came and stayed in her home. Her daddy and brothers opened their home to me. Kenna would sit and play her guitar on the front porch of her house, and I would sit there most evenings and listen, letting the strum of the strings soothe me. I don't know if she knows that she is the one who got me through the loss of my mother or the guilt that I felt for not protecting her. I regretfully never told or thanked Kenna for this.

As I sat in my truck, letting the guilt consume me from so many years ago, I shivered from still feeling Kenna's hands in mine that night, months after I had broken down, broke from the pain of losing my mother and the guilt of failing her. I was sitting on the steps of the front porch, and Kenna was playing her guitar. The sound of her fingers hitting the strings made the most soothing sound.

Something inside me broke, and my eyes filled with tears. The tears just would not stop. With my elbows on my knees, I dropped my head into my hands to hide the tears from Kenna. I didn't want her to see me weak or broken because that's what I felt: broken. She reached up and pulled my hands from my face. As she intertwined her hands with mine, I peeked up into the most beautiful emerald green eyes.

That was the moment, the moment I knew she was my perfection. I knew there was no way I could have her. I would only be able to admire her from afar. I pulled my hands from hers and cupped her beautiful face. I felt it when she leaned into my hand. As I slowly slid my hand from her face, I tried to stop myself, but my thumb rubbed across her bottom lip. It took all my power not to kiss her, but I succeeded. Once my thumb ran across her lip and down her chin, I stood and walked away and right past Finn, who was watching from the front door.

Finn and I never spoke of that moment, and I don't believe he ever told Conor. Conor isn't thinking like Finn. He would break my neck if I ever did anything with his baby sister. I may be one of the best fighters around now, but everything I've learned I've learned from the family who took me in. Even though he is my best friend, my brother, he would not think twice about ending me if I did anything with his baby sister.

The last time I left this mobile home park, I had lost the most important woman in my life. Now, pulling out years later, I vowed I would make that motherfucker who put his hands on my Mackenna pay. Yes, she is mine, even if I can't have her. She has always been mine. Tearing onto the road, I thought how good it would feel to beat that motherfucker, how it would feel to cause the same pain to him that I know he did to Kenna. How to scare him to the point of pissing himself. The anger was burning through me. My car rang with a call as I turned left onto my road. Finn's name appeared on the dash.

"Finn, what's up?" I asked firmly.

"Dude, I know you. I know this is eating at you right now, plus I saw the newbie's face you used as a punching bag at the gym," Finn stated.

"I can't right now, Finn. I'm about to—"

Finn jumped in before I could finish.

"Dude, I know how you feel about Ken. I've watched you for years pining over her, asshole. Plus, with your past, I know you are ready to fuck someone up."

I said nothing. Honestly, what could I say? I knew that Finn knew, but there was no way I was saying it out loud.

Finn started speaking again, "If you are going to come tonight, I need you to keep yourself together. I don't think Conor could handle the fact that you are in love with our sister."

"Fuck, Finn, I'm not in love with Kenna. You don't know what you are talking about," not believing the words coming out of my mouth.

9

MACKENNA

Taking a deep breath, Chrissy turned the knob of the front door of my family home. I followed her into the place where I grew up, the place I hadn't returned to since my daddy passed away. I looked around to see the furniture my brothers had replaced, but other than that, everything was the same. The living room, where I spent so many times harassing my brothers, still had all the family photos hanging on the wall.

Where there was once a small, flowered sofa, now sat a large brown leather sectional that looked like you would sink into. Across the room was the big bay window that I can remember brought in the bright sunlight. The curtains that were once faded white had been replaced with new bright white curtains that hung all the way to the dark hardwood floors, which I knew had been refinished since the last time I was there.

As we walked toward the kitchen, I took notice of the massive television that hung on one of the walls. As I passed the staircase, I could not help but look up and wonder if my room was still the same. I mentally stated that I would have to go up and check. Entering the kitchen, I was taken aback by the changes. What was once an outdated kitchen was now sleek and modern. There was absolutely no way my brothers designed this kitchen.

"Do you like it?" Chrissy asked.

"You designed this, didn't you?" I asked her.

"I hope you don't mind, but Conor and Finn asked for my help."

"It is beautiful," I said because, well, it was.

Black cabinets lined the back wall with a massive, probably the biggest stainless-steel refrigerator I'd ever seen. A stainless-steel farmer sink overlooked the yard. A massive black island sat in the middle of the room. The counters were the whitest marble that brightened the space.

Three large pendant lights hung above the island. Steel stools lined the island. With a quick count, I saw there were eight of them. That was how large the island was. The wall to the kitchen and dining room was no longer there, leaving an open dining and kitchen combo.

They had replaced the old dining table with an ebony-stained farmer's table with four steel chairs on each side and a tall white back chair at each end of the table. There was no chandelier, just recessed lighting that lined the ceiling, making the room bright. I could hardly believe this was the home I grew up in; it was so different.

Finn came around the island and dropped his arm over my shoulder, bringing me in for a hug, but instead of letting go, he held me in tight with a kiss to my head. He asked how I was holding up. Finn was always the levelheaded one. He could always keep his cool, and even though he was a big guy covered in tattoos that could scare the average person, in actuality, he was kind and caring.

Don't get me wrong. Inside he is raging with anger and would like very much to break the man in half that hurt his baby sister. It is a very good thing Brad lives in another state, although I would not put it past Conor to jump on a plane and snap Brad in half.

"Where's Con?" I asked.

"He is outside manning the grill. We need to keep him busy, or he is going to kill someone," Finn stated, like he knew what I was just thinking.

I noticed as Finn was hugging me that Chrissy had slipped outside. I'm not sure what's with those two or when they became such close friends, but I made a mental note to ask her.

Finally slipping out of my brother's embrace, I turned and jumped when I saw him. I never heard the front door open and close, but at some point, he entered and was leaning against the door jamb staring. Ryan was very tall, over a foot taller than me. He was wearing worn-out ripped jeans with a white t-shirt that revealed his black tattoos underneath.

I had seen Ryan with no shirt on plenty of times, so I know he was rock solid under that white t-shirt with a very deep V.

I licked my lips to give them moisture, staring where I knew that V had begun. I brought my eyes up to his full lips and his crooked nose from being broken a few times. I then met his deep brown eyes that had these golden specks in them. His eyes had always been stunning. His brown hair was so short now from clearly a fresh buzz cut. Ryan was always clean-shaven, but now he had a tight brown beard that I wish was scratching my inner thighs.

I hadn't seen Ryan since my daddy's funeral. He sat beside me with his hand on my thigh, not a care in the world that Brad was on the other side of me. I think back to that moment a lot. Brad was my boyfriend, but Ryan was my soul. He just didn't know it.

I was sure in his mind that he was trying to comfort me like I had comforted him when his mother was murdered in her home by a man she was in love with. Looking back at him, I saw his brown eyes burning through me. I immediately went back to the night we sat on our front porch and grabbed hold of his hands and held them. That night I saw that same fire in his eyes. He came so close to me I could feel his breath on my skin.

I thought for sure he was going to kiss me, but he didn't. He got up and left. My heart went with him that night and has always been with him; he just had no idea he was holding it. Ryan stared at me for so long I could feel the electricity run through my body. God, how could he do that to me with just a look? He had no idea the hold he has on me.

A few moments later, he straightened up and started to walk toward me slowly. I didn't even see Finn leave my side, but he did because that was Finn; he trusted Ryan. He knew Ryan would protect me with his life, so Finn backed away and gave Ryan the space to come to me. As he got closer, I could feel the goosebumps forming on my arms.

He reached out and put his hand on my cheek, my bruised cheek. Then he stared directly into my eyes. It felt like he would never speak, but finally, he muttered, "I'm going to fucking kill him."

That sentence snapped me back to reality. He was not going to hug me or welcome me. Ryan was only seeing me as his best friend's sister, the family he needed to protect. I pushed his hand away and flatly stated, "I'm fine," as I walked away, not looking back at him, just exiting out the slider to head to the backyard. Both Conor and Chrissy stood by the grill. I placed a hand on Chrissy's shoulder and leaned in to kiss Conor on the cheek.

My ribs were still bruised, so I moved into a sitting position with a squeak, trying my best to not show anyone my pain. Chrissy put her hand out for me to grab in an effort to help me up. We walked hand and hand back into the kitchen and took a seat at the table. With Conor at the head and Chrissy in the first seat with me beside her. On the other side of Conor sat Finn and Ryan next to him directly across from me.

I kept my head down, but I felt all the eyes on me, especially the deep brown, almost golden eyes that set my insides on fire. "Don't look at him, don't look at him, don't look at him," I kept saying to myself, but the urge was too strong, and I lifted my eyes up to those eyes staring directly into mine.

"Kenna, we can grab your stuff in the morning

and bring it back here," Conor said, pulling me from Ryan's glare.

"What? No. I'm staying with Chrissy." Turning my neck to look at Chrissy, I said, "I thought you were all right with me staying with you?"

Chrissy peeked at Conor, then back at me. "Of course, you can stay as long as you want. Conor, she is fine staying with me."

"Fuck, Kenna, this is your home," he said. "You should be with us. We're the ones to take care of—"

"What the hell are you talking about, Con? I'm a grown woman. I can take care of myself, and I'm staying with Chrissy," I stated in a sharp tone.

His fork slammed to his plate and lifted his head, his usual ocean blue eyes now dark.

"I can see that," he said.

My face snapped in his direction and then around to the table to everyone just bowing their heads. As I stood, scraping the chair legs on the hardwood floors, putting my hands on the table, and leaning over Chrissy, I glared directly at Conor.

"Fuck you," I said. "You're an asshole."

I turned and ran to the front of the house, opening the front door and slamming it on my way out. I dropped to the front step, hands covering my eyes, and began to cry. I can't believe Conor just said that he thinks I'm weak, that I can't take care of myself.

10

RYAN

"Fuck, Conor. Did you really just say that?" I asked, looking over at Conor and slamming my fist to the table.

"Shit, I didn't mean that. I'm so fucking mad that I just spit it out. I want her home. I want her here. I want to make sure she's safe," Conor said defeated.

I pushed out of my chair and looking around the table I said, "I got her. Let me talk to her."

Finn, who said nothing while Kenna was sitting at the table, looked up. "If anyone could talk to her about this, it's you."

I squeezed both Finn and Conor's shoulder as I walked by. They know I love them, and I would do anything for Kenna. They are my everything. I took a few deep breathes as I made my way to the front porch seeing her through the window sitting on the top step with her hands burying her face. I quietly closed the door and made my way to her wanting so badly to wrap her up in my arms and keep her there. That was not an option, so I placed my hand on her delicate shoulder and sat beside her.

"Kenna, he didn't mean it. He's just worried about you. Conor and Finn both love you and want only the best for you," I said in a low voice.

She didn't lift her face to look at me just kept it buried in her hands. I could hear the faintest sniffle telling me she was crying. I lowered my hand from her shoulder to her back wanting to pull her closer to me, but I stopped myself and slowly rubbed my hand up and down her back.

"Want me to take you back to Chrissy's" I asked. "Maybe, try for dinner another night."

I know her, her whole life she has been a stubborn smartass, there was no way she was going back in there to face her brothers.

If I were not looking so closely, I would've missed her nodding her head in response. "Come on, I will take."

It was a silent drive back to Chrissy's which was fine with me I needed to pull myself together and not drag her home with me to keep her safe. I parked the truck and jumped out to run to the other side.

When I got there Kenna being Kenna was already

out of the truck. At that moment with the moonlight now shining and her eyes glossy from tears I had to, I had to touch her. I cautiously placed my hand on her arm and then with a mind of its own it slid down and into her hand.

We walked without saying a word. Finally, when we reached the door, she glanced up at me. "Thank you, Ryan, there was no way I was going back in there."

Damn. I just winked at her letting her know I knew she wasn't. *I fucking winked at her. Jesus, what's wrong with me? A fucking wink. I'm pathetic.*

When she turned to open the door, I did something I knew I should not do I grabbed her arm. Kenna pulled hard out of my soft grip and swung around.

I quickly put both hands in the air. "I'm sorry, so sorry. I didn't mean to scare you."

At that moment I saw the fear in her eyes that quickly turned to sadness. I took a step back and said, "I would never hurt you, Kenna, never."

"I know you wouldn't I ju—"

She didn't finish the statement she just stared straight ahead at me. When I found out what happened to Kenna I thought about the time frame and something came to my mind.

"Kenna, when did he hit you?" I asked but she

didn't answer me she just looked into my eyes and then down to her feet. I softly grabbed her by the chin and lifted her to face me. "Kenna, when did he hit you?" I asked again dreading the answer.

It was soft but I heard her say, "Friday morning."

She knew at that moment that I knew why he had hit her.

"It was my text, wasn't it?" I asked.

"It is over now. It doesn't matter. I'm home, far away from him," she stated firmly.

I stepped closer to her. "It was my text . . ."

I wasn't asking this time.

"Yes," she said.

"Kenna, I'm so sorry." She tried to look down, but I held her chin to look directly into my eyes. With another step forward, I stated again, "I'm so sorry."

I was so close to her now, one more step would close the distance. I can't, I shouldn't, it didn't matter what my mind was saying, my body moved. I took that last step closing the distance. I lifted her chin a little more and whispered, "Kenna."

I felt her breath on me. I felt her chest beating against mine. I can't, I should not don't do it I kept shouting in my head but then I heard her whisper, "Ryan," her breath hitting my mouth.

Fuck . . .

My lips collided with hers, one hand moving to

the back of her neck. Against my better judgment, I opened my mouth sliding my tongue over her bottom lip. She opened up to me. Our tongues collided.

"Fuck, Kenna. We can't. I say into her mouth."

She said nothing Kenna just wrapped her hands around my shoulders and pulled me to her tighter. I could feel the cut on her mouth open and the blood in my mouth. It didn't matter, are tongues just continued their war. My other hand wrapped around her lower back, and she arched, lifting her leg to my hip.

Holy shit. I can't believe this is happening.

My hand around her neck dropped to her ass as the one on her lower back did the same. I lifted and when I did, she wrapped her legs around me. I can't, I should not. I pulled back "Kenna, we can't be doing this."

"We can." She again pulled me closer, blood on both our mouths. It didn't matter. We kissed again, opening up to each other. I could feel the heat coming from her core and my dick pressing hard against the zipper of my jeans. Then I felt her arch again pushing her core against my zipper.

"Fuck," I grunted into her mouth.

If I didn't stop right now, I would never stop. She tasted like a mixture of blood and sugar, and I could not get enough. We were both fighting a battle, but this battle I could not win this. I pulled back once more releasing my hands from her ass. She lowered her legs to stand.

As I backed away, I said one last time, "Kenna, we can't."

I could see she was breathless and a little wobbly on her feet, so I reached my hand out to stable her, but she pushed it away. "Are you fucking serious?"

"Kenna, please."

"Ryan, we can!"

"I can't." I started to turn away. "Go inside and lock the door," I said, then walked away.

11

MACKENNA

"Ugh." Rolling myself over, I dragged a pillow over my head.

The morning sun bright in my eyes through the large window that takes up most of the bedroom wall. My head aches and thighs hurt from wrapping them so tight around Ryan's waist.

Pushing the pillow harder into my face I said, "Fuck. I'm so stupid. What was I thinking?"

I kissed Ryan. Oh, my god, I pretty much mauled him.

Removing the pillow from my face and rolling over to lay flat I punch the mattress. I stared up at the ceiling focusing on the ceiling fan replaying the event that happened just hours ago. My lips touching his, our tongues in a battle his hands on my body my legs wrapped around him and oh god the heat, there was so much heat.

"It wasn't just me," I whisper to myself.

He was into it too, I felt it.

Rubbing a hand over my face I got up from the bed wrapped myself in the robe that Chrissy left on the bed for me. She loves a comfy robe always has, so I was not surprised she left me one. She would always tell me that a comfy robe made up for the lack of a man's arms wrapped around her.

She was crazy but I loved her.

Tying the robe around my waist, I reach for the door and open it to silence. It was still early, only seven thirty, so I knew Chrissy was still here.

"Fuck, I need coffee." I walk over to the coffee maker on the counter.

Chrissy was old school. No K-Cup maker for her. She likes to brew a full pot.

"Need coffee, huh?" I jump at the sound of Conor's voice.

A yelp passed my lips. Startled, I jumped. Turning around, I hit my hip on the counter.

"Shit," I hissed. "You scared me. Wait? What are you doing here?" I asked

Conor leaned forward on the sofa he was taking up space on. "I came to see you, but I didn't want to wake you."

"Where is Chrissy?" I asked looking around the apartment.

"She went to take a shower," Conor rose from the sofa and made his way over to me.

He pulled out a stool to sit on the island.

"When the hell did you get here," I asked.

"I came back last night to talk to you, but the door to the room was quiet. So, I didn't want to wake you," he said.

I poured my cup of coffee. For a moment, I was thankful that things didn't go any further with Ryan because if Conor had caught us, he would have murdered both of us.

"I want to talk to you. Can you come sit with me?" he asked, after adding a little cream to my coffee, then returning it to the fridge.

I moved around the island and sat down beside my brother.

His head was bowed and focused on his coffee. I knew he felt guilty. I knew he was hurting for me. I knew he was worried—they all were.

I put a sympathetic hand on his arm and squeeze just a little, enough for him to know I was here.

"Ugh, Kenna, I'm sorry for what I said to you last night. I didn't mean it. When I saw you walk into my office yesterday with bruises, these bruises." He placed his hand on my cheek. "Fuck, it killed me."

144

I leaned my cheek into his hand and smiled at my big brother. "I know it did. I love you too."

"I'm your big brother. I'm supposed to protect you . . . I should be keeping you safe," he said in a defeated tone.

"Conor, you were not there to—"

"Fuck, Kenna, I know. I'm sorry. I'm so sorry."

I hadn't heard Conor's voice crack like that since he was a teenager.

"Conor, no. That isn't what I mean. You're my brother. I love you. I really do. But you can't keep thinking you're going to protect me all my life. I moved away. I made that choice. I left home, so I could take care of myself, and become independent." I took Conor's hand from my cheek and placed it into mine. "I'm okay now. I'm here away from Brad. I'm safe."

The pain in my brother's face was breaking my heart. Here was this giant of a man at least compared to me. Big and strong. He was a fighter and a trainer but most important, he was compassionate. Above all else, he was a gentle giant who would never hurt a woman.

Holding my hand, he looked at me. "When did it start?"

Not wanting to answer that question, I glanced down and blew into my coffee to avoid answering.

"Micky, answer me, please."

"It wasn't always that way. When I met Brad, he was a charmer, romantic. He would buy me flowers, take me to dinner in these quaint restaurants. He would hold me hand, give me his jacket when I was cold. He would open the car door for me. Then little things started to change. I can't tell you exactly when, it was very subtle. He would get jealous over the stupidest thing."

"What else?"

"He would make a comment about the way I dressed and thought I was seeking attention."

"That's bullshit."

"He would make comments here and there about my writing and how I should be looking for a real job," I said. "Conor, you know me. I've got a smart mouth and I had no problem calling him out on his shit."

Silence fell between us.

"Then one night, I called him an asshole." I glanced down again. "And, well, he smacked me."

Conor growled out a breath but didn't interrupt me.

Now that I had started talking, I was going to purge it all. I had to get it all out of me.

"I swear, I left him when he did that. I kicked him out of my apartment. He left for about a week,

146

and then he started texting me. Telling me how sorry he was and that he would never do that again.

I toyed with my cup.

"At some point, after numerous texts and attempts to see me, I broke down and went to see him. It was like when we first started dating. He was sweet and caring. Eventually, I made the mistake and forgave him."

"Fuck," he whispered without judgement.

"Once that happened, he had control," I said. "I wish I could explain how it happened, but I just can't. Somehow, I lost myself. His words beat me down and my self-esteem was gone. One night after a fight we had, I was in a group text with you and Finn . . . we were joking around. You guys were texting about girls you were with or hooking up with. Do you remember that?"

Conor just shrugged.

"Anyway, Brad saw a text that came through about a sexy ass, and he thought Ryan was texting me."

"Fuck," Conor interrupted with a growling.

I squeezed his hand to try and calm him. "That night was bad, Conor. It was the start of things really getting bad. He smacked me so hard that I flew off the sofa and landed on the floor. He got on top of me and hit me again, and then he dragged me to the bedroom, and he—"

"Stop! Fucking stop," Conor snapped, throwing the stool he just jumped off across the room, hitting the coffee table. "Did he, did he . . ."

Conor couldn't finish, and I knew what he was asking. He was asking if he had raped me that night. At the time, I was so broken inside that I just let him, and I didn't believe it was rape given that we were in a relationship, for god's sake, but now, I knew I could admit what it was.

"Yes, he raped me," I whispered. More tears formed in my eyes and ran down my cheeks.

"Kenna? Conor? Is everything okay?" Chrissy asked with concern.

Neither one of us noticed Chrissy had entered the room.

Conor looked between us and asked, "Are you going to work?"

Chrissy immediately took the hint and grabbed her purse and keys. "Yeah. I'm heading out now." She looked at me with sympathy in her eyes. "Uhm, Kenna, do you want me to stay? I can call into work."

"No, n-no. It's okay. We're good."

Without another word, Chrissy left, leaving us alone with this bomb I had dropped in the middle of her kitchen. Neither one of us said a word. Conor just stood at the slider, looking out at the palm trees that lined the building.

I wasn't sure how long we remained silent, but at some point, Conor made his way over to where I stood and wrapped his arms around me. He held me. Conor didn't ask any more questions, nor did I continue my purge. Instead, I just let him hold me until he dragged me to the sofa, holding the rest of the morning.

By around noon, my stomach started to make noises.

Conor chuckle. "Hungry?"

"Mmm," I hummed.

"How about you go get dressed and we go grab lunch?" Conor asked.

I was not about to argue all I had was a half a cup of coffee I was dehydrated and hungry. I jumped up not saying a word ran to get dressed and quickly brushed my teeth and hair. We were out the door in less than fifteen minutes.

As we pulled into a diner across from the gym, I could not help but look over to see if Ryan's truck was in the lot. I was not surprised when I saw it in the same spot he parked in when we were teenagers. I had to laugh to myself that Ryan is a creature of habit I can guarantee he still wakes up most mornings and goes for a five-mile run.

When Ryan stayed with us, I would set my alarm every morning and sneak downstairs and wait for him. He would come down in his shorts, tank, socks, and sneakers in hand and say the same thing to me every time.

"Why are you up so early, little Kenna." That was the big joke in our house—my height.

I was surrounded by tall men from Daddy to my brothers to Ryan.

"Come on, let's eat," Conor said, knocking me out of my Ryan dream.

We spent the lunch, mostly in silence, but with a few childhood stories all including of course Ryan. My mind kept wondering to last night.

I swear I saw the hunger in Ryan's eyes. I could have sworn he wanted me as much as I wanted him.

Turning to look out the window of the diner, I caught Finn and Ryan walking across the street straight toward the diner.

"Oh, fuck," I said to myself.

Oh, fuck. Oh, fuck.

I must have been making a face because Conor asked, "What's wrong?"

Before I could answer the bell above the diner door jingled and then at that moment everything stopped. His eyes met mine and I swear I was about to have a panic attack. My mouth went dry, and my hands got sweaty as I was trying to calm my breathing. Thank god, Connor had turned around and wasn't looking at me. But Ryan, he was looking at me. His eyes stayed directly on mine.

Don't pass out. Don't fucking pass out, I chanted in my mind.

"Micky, are you okay?" Finn asked when he reached the table.

"Uh-huh. Um, yeah. I'm good," I said trying to be believable.

Finn slid onto the same side as Conor while Ryan continued to look at me. "Kenna, can you slide down?"

Oh god. Oh, my god. He's going to sit beside me.

I slid over and continued the little *'Oh god. Oh, my god'* chant in my mind.

The booth seat groaned with his weight, and his knee hit mine. Instead of moving, he kept it there, leaning against mine.

Yup. I'm gonna pass out. I just knew it. *There is no possible way I'm gonna make it through this lunch without passing out.*

"So, what's new?" Finn asked.

I froze in place. *Oh, my god. Not here. Not now.* Of course, as with everything else in my life, the bomb was about to not only drop, but implode, crash, and burn.

12

RYAN

I knew Kenna would be there—knew they were going to tell her—and I knew she would freak when she found out. I wasn't about to let her learn the news alone.

When Finn had told me that he was running across the street to have lunch with Conor and Kenna, I jumped out of the octagon, unwrapped my hands, then ran to catch up.

"I'm starving. I'll join you," I said.

Finn just gave me an eye roll. "Yeah. Sure, okay."

He didn't have to tell me what was going to happen because I already knew.

What I wasn't expecting was my reaction when I entered the diner.

She was like a magnet. The moment I entered the

building, my eyes flew to her. I could divert my gaze even if I tried.

But then again, my eyes always sought her out. It has always been that way, and that would never change.

When Finn slid in with Conor, my heart skipped a beat. Again, like a magnet, my knee went against hers. I fought not to put my hand on her thigh. It took every ounce of strength I had.

Once the waitress approached, Conor, Finn, and I ordered the grilled chicken salad because we all knew we'd be heading back to the gym. Kenna, she went for a burger and fries. Of course, we all stole a few of her fries. And for the food trespasses, we each got a dirty look in turn.

I didn't miss that her glance in my direction lingered a little longer. After a few bites of food, Finn cleared his throat, and we all looked up at him.

"Micky," he started. "We need to talk to you."

"Oh fuck," she said. "What? Please, I don't know if I can handle any more bad news."

"I don't think it's bad news," Finn said. "But it may be a little of a shock to you."

Kenna put the burger down and wiped her hands on her yoga pants. Immediately, my thoughts went to the way her ass looked in those pants.

Dammit. Stopping thinking like that. With a subtle shake of my head, I pushed the thought out of my mind, then glanced over at Finn, waiting for him to continue.

"So, you turn twenty-five soon," he said.

"Yeah," she spat out. "I'm well aware, Finn. Next month actually, in case you forgot the date, it's October twenty-third."

"Ha-ha. I know the date, you little shit," he went on, "well, I think you should know what's coming on your birthday."

"Okay. What?" Kenna looked around the booth, wondering what the hell was going on.

There is a trust set up for you," said Conor. He was the one handling everything.

"What are you talking about?" Kenna asked.

I knew about the trust because Conor and Finn had told me everything. Although, I would never tell them I think about their sister laid out on my bed.

Nope, not telling them that.

"The house the gym Dad's estate . . . The house is in all our names, the gym, well you own a third of it."

"What the fuck are you talking about? You guys have the gym I've never been a part of that." Kenna said Dumbfounded.

Conor continued "Dad left it all in all our names No access until we're twenty-five. Finn and I, well, we were already twenty-five when dad passed but you weren't. Now you are and you have a third of everything." Kenna's eyes grew wide.

"There is an account in your name. Finn and I've been depositing into it since dad's death. We made quarterly deposits with the profits of the gym."

I had to turn my head away from Kenna and smile because she was about to learn something major.

"Kenna, we train professional fighters in our gym, do you understand how much they make a fight?" Finn asked.

"No, I never paid any attention to that stuff. You know that I just wanted my music." Kenna said.

"Well, they make a lot, not just a lot but a shit ton. The gym gets a percentage of each fight. Not only that but we manage the fighters. Our gym isn't just a little neighborhood gym. Fighters come from all over the world here to train with us." Conor said proudly.

Kenna eyed me trying to take everything in.

I smiled at her and waited as Conor went on, "The gym is worth millions, Kenna."

Of course, Conor chose the moment she was taking a sip of her water to say millions.

Kenna spit the water out in utter shock. "What!"

With her hand over her mouth and her eyes

wide, she glanced around the table first at Conor then at Finn finally landing on me.

I could not help but smirk and nod my head. "Do you think I choose to get bruises like this for nothing?"

Realizing what I had said, and the current bruise that showed on her beautiful face, I reached over and put my hand on her thigh.

"Kenna, I'm sorry I didn't mean it like that."

Looking down at my hand, she said, "Stop! It is all right. Everyone needs to stop being sorry. It happened and it is over now. Let's just move on. Brad isn't here. He can't hurt me anymore." She paused a moment, then added, "Holy shit. I can't believe this is happening, but I don't understand why I'm just finding out about this trust. Now." She studied Finn and Conor, trying to understand. "Why didn't you tell me?"

No one answered Kenna. We all sat silently, letting her digest the news she was just given.

"You're telling me that there's an account with my name that has money? Not a little but a lot? Are you fucking kidding me right now? I spent the last year of my life giving half my tip money to Jeff so Brad could not take it. And all along, I would've had money to get away from him?"

We all stared at each other as if unsure of what to say.

"I lived in a shitty fucking apartment in one of the worst neighborhoods and there is money in an account for me. You could have told me. You should have told me! What the fuck is wrong with you guys. I lived in hell with no money and a man who fucking enjoyed hitting me. I could have run sooner. Hell, I could have come home sooner."

Kenna turns to face me and with both hands, pushes me.

"Move," she yelled.

I instantly jumped from the booth and Kenna pushed her way out. I stayed standing beside her, watching as she faced her brothers, pointing a finger at them.

"I can't fucking believe you wouldn't tell me. You should've told me. I'm leaving! Don't follow me. Don't call me. Don't text me. Leave me alone. I can't look at any of you." Then she turned and ran out of the diner.

13

MACKENNA

Christmas Time

With Michael Bublé's Christmas album playing, I begin opening the ornaments I bought for my very first Christmas tree that I had bought for my new place.

Yup, I thought, *the past few weeks have been crazy.*

I learned that my daddy had a trust made for me before he passed away. I gained access to the money on my twenty-fifth birthday. It's hard to believe a few months ago, I was secretly giving money to one of my best friends for him to hold so I could get away from my abusive boyfriend.

Now, here I am, twenty-five, with money to afford my own apartment, money to furnish the new apartment, and money to do oh, so much more.

Here, today, I'm decorating my very own two-bedroom apartment. Excitement bubbled up inside me. It has a humungous kitchen with marble countertops. *I can't lie.* I splurged on a few things, including a large Christmas tree with tons of decorations.

I've settled into a new normal back home. I made some contacts with local bands and helped a few write new songs. I'm back to journals strewn about all over my apartment, so I can write whenever something comes to mind. I walk to the park around the corner most days and sit with my guitar and write. I've yet to write something for myself, but I'm enjoying writing for other local artists for the time being. I'm super excited to start a new gig.

Recently, I signed up with a local production company that books gigs for local artists. Soon, I'll begin traveling to local bars, clubs, and resorts to play for mostly tourists.

I would like to say everything was going great but that would be a lie.

The lunch I had with my brothers and Ryan, the one where I learned about the trust and a third ownership in the gym and family home, didn't end the way they had expected. Looking back, I wish I could have changed my reaction.

Hell, I don't even know why I ended up reacting the way I did.

At the time, everything that happened with Brad was still very fresh. I lost a lot of who I was during that relationship. So, as I sat in that booth and listened to Conor and Finn tell me about the money, the gym, and our family home, I lost it. At first, I sat there in shock, I couldn't help but get angry. No, pissed off that they were hiding things from me.

The money could have helped me.

We're supposed to be family. We should be having each other's backs.

But sitting there, I realized one thing. We knew very little about each other. Our lives had changed over the years, and we had drifted apart. That realization made me angry. Angry at them and angry at myself.

Moving home was the first step of taking my life back. But finding out . . . knowing that there were *these* secrets between my brothers and me, made me I snap.

I took all my anger out on them and poor Ryan who sat beside me. I said mean and hurtful things to each of them. I shouted at them in the middle of a diner. Patrons watched me throwing my hands around and yelling about how they were supposed to be my family and shouldn't keep secrets from me.

From there, it only got worse. It progressed to me shouting about how they weren't there for me. How they didn't help me or protect me. I'm not sure why I would blame them for any of my suffering when I made it a point to hide it from all of them.

The truth is I blame myself.

I blamed myself for being stupid, for staying with such a man, for not leaving sooner.

Most of all I was angry that I was absolutely in love with the person sitting beside me in that booth that day and had never been able to tell him.

Since that lunch, we have spoken very little.

My conversations with Conor and Ryan have only been about the trust, the gym, and our family home. I've kept my distance from all of them, trying to get my life and myself together.

I know Conor and Finn both feel incredibly guilty for waiting to tell me, and I know they feel like they failed me—that they didn't feel like they protected me.

The truth is, I'm not theirs to protect.

I shouldn't have made them feel that way. I knew then that I needed to face them and make things right but instead, I've avoided them.

Ryan has tried to reach out. He has texted and called, but again, I've acted like a coward and haven't answered him.

Well, that's until last night.

After dragging the delivered box inside my apartment—the very large box holding a humongous artificial tree—I pour a glass of wine, and then a second glass shortly after that one. Once I was on my third glass, I stared at his contact information on my phone.

After several minutes of taping the side of my phone, turning it on and off, I opened the text messages Ryan had sent me over the past few weeks.

> Ryan: I'm sorry I wasn't there to protect you.

> Ryan: Are you okay?

> Ryan: Kenna, I'm so sorry.

> Ryan: Please, answer me, Kenna.

> Ryan: I'm worried. Please let me know if you're okay.

I scrolled through weeks of texts that he had sent with absolutely no reply from me.

Ugh. I'm so stupid. I should've just answered him.

I finally came to the end of his message, and read the last text Ryan sent, which was over a week ago.

> Ryan: I love you.

My hands began to shake. I had to place the wine glass on the table. Holding the phone with both hands, I watched the words on my phone bounce around, as my phone went from one hand to another, shaking all the while.

Wait. Did he just admit he loves me?

I hit the reply button and quickly typed out a single reply.

> ME: What?

I saw he read the text immediately, but instead of the bubbles appearing on the phone, telling me he was typing back, my phone rang. Startled, and not expecting an actual call from him, I jumped.

The phone bounced out of my hands and onto the sofa beside me.

Quickly, grabbed it and swiped to answer. I didn't say anything, instead, I just waited for him to speak.

"Kenna. Are you there? he asked. "Please talk to me."

After taking a slow deep breath, I said, "Yes, I'm here."

Silence hit the line. It was as if we were both waiting for the other to speak.

Not wanting to beat around the bush, I went right for it. "You said you loved me."

When I said the words, my heart started to beat so hard, I swear Ryan could hear it through the phone.

My hands started to sweat, forcing me to grip the phone a little harder so it wouldn't slip out of my fingers.

Was he about to tell me how he felt? To express his emotions—feelings I'd waited years to hear spoken.

"Of course, I do. You are my family," he said.

And just like that, I deflated like a hot air balloon with a hole.

It felt like a knife was going right into my heart. It hurt so bad.

My mind drifted to the time he drove me to Chrissy's, of when we kissed.

Shit, we did more than kiss.

I thought for sure he felt something more for me. I honestly thought he was feeling the same thing for me.

How stupid am I?

He was just a guy hooking up with his best friends' little sister. Well, until he realized Conor would kill him.

Fuck. I'm the stupidest person alive.

I stayed quiet, letting Ryan have the preverbal floor.

"Kenna." He sighed. "What happened between us, well, that can't happen. You know that, don't you?" he asked.

His words deflated me some more.

I lowered myself into the sofa. Squeezing my eyes tight, I fought to hold back the liquid emotions. I didn't want to let a single tear release.

Several agonizing seconds ticked by, which felt more like an eternity, and I didn't answer.

"Kenna," he whispered.

I had to speak. I had to say something. I didn't want him to know how deep his words had cut, how he was affecting me.

"Of course, Ryan. I know that can't happen." I bite the inside of my mouth, not wanting to say the words wanting on the tip of my tongue. "It was a total mistake. I don't know what I was thinking that night." With the words exiting my mouth, a single tear rolled down my cheek.

Quickly, I wiped it away.

"Hey," Ryan said. "I heard you got a new place." It was as if nothing had ever happened between us— not a kiss, no touch, no moment of carnal desire. "I heard you got a new place."

So, this is my new life, huh? Suppressing my feelings and pretending I feel nothing for him.

"I did. I moved in a week ago," I said, trying to sound happy. "I would love to see it. Can I come by tomorrow? Maybe, we can get lunch." He paused long enough to draw in a breath of air. "Let's get past this Kenna, so we can still be like we always were. Okay?"

Yeah, right. Once again, I fought back the raw liquid emotions burning my eyes with unshed tears. *Like we always were.*

I don't know if I could ever be that way again. But I couldn't just let him go. In all honesty, I couldn't imagine Ryan, not in my life. He has been there through so much.

"Yeah, that sounds good. I will text you the address. Come by around noon," I spoke quickly, trying to end the call as fast as I could.

The moment I hung up, I gulped down another glass of wine, then placed my head on one of the throw pillows.

Now, in the hazy fog of Christmas, I sat unpacking the decorations and listening to Michael Bublé in the background, trying to mentally prepare myself.

14

MACKENNA

In the friend zone. A sigh left my lips.

Soon, Ryan would arrive to see his *friend's* apartment, actually, his best friends' little sister's apartment. He wasn't coming to see the woman he loved.

Nope. I'm the friend. That's me. The fuckin' friend—the one who loves him.

Shit. I needed to pull it together and bury those feeling deep, as deep as I could.

The thump, thump, thump of the door made me jump.

I bumped into the coffee table, knocking a bunch of ornaments onto the floor.

"Fuck," I said, turning to head to the door. Halfway there, I tripped over a pile of Christmas lights strung across the middle of the floor. My foot got, and I hopped on one leg, shaking the snared foot. Seconds later, I slammed into a corner of the coffee table.

"Fuck. Fuck. Fuck," I snap. "Jesus. Get off my foot."

My foot touched the ground, and the spiny light covers bit into my arc like grass burs or pronged, thorny stickers. The painful impact had me hopping around one-footed again.

"Shit. I'm coming!" Finally, I got my foot free, then tossed the lights behind me.

Fuck. I groaned. *Please, don't let them be broken.*

Another thump, thump at the door, drew my eye to the entry. I stop abruptly where I stood, took a deep calming breath, then straighten myself out.

"Kenna," I whispered to myself. "Get a fucking grip."

I lowered my hand to the doorknob, gripped it, then opening the door. And there he was, looking fucking incredible in a fitted long sleeve grey shirt and jeans that fit him perfectly. His beard has got fuller since the last time I had seen him and damn, if it didn't look incredible on him.

His golden-brown eyes trapped me and drew me. The side of his mouth jerked into a small smirk.

Damn. Heat pooled between my legs, and I squeeze my thighs together to relieve the building pressure.

In his hands, he held two large coffees. "I got you a coffee."

Shit. I can do this. I can pretend I feel nothing for this gorgeous man. The memory of the kiss we shared played on a never-ending loop. *I can and will keep it together.*

Moving aside to let him enter, I smacked my arm on the door. "Fuck."

Yup. I'm doing a great job holding it together.

"Ugh. Come on in," I say as I rub the pain from my arm.

"I brought you a coffee. I hope there is enough cream in there for you." He hands me the cup with steam still coming from the little whole in the cover.

I smile grabbing the cup from him still feeling the pain in my arm. "Thanks."

Ryan walks further into my place, and I turn and shut the door, shaking my head at my craziness.

Looking around Ryan said, "This place is fantastic, Kenna. You did a great job."

I really did I loved my new place. It was a very similar layout to Chrissy's apartment. Except I had higher ceilings. This unit had dark hardwood floors with light grey walls.

The Kitchen had cabinets that were also grey but about two shades darker with white marble countertops. The large island was a light blue with the same white marble tops. I did purchase white stools that lined one side of the island. Plus, I found a beautiful farmer's table.

It was smaller than my brothers and sat six people comfortably. I had it painted the same pale blue as the island with white chairs. For the living room, I went with an L-Shaped sofa that was a darker grey but with white throw pillows and white blankets draped on the end.

The coffee table was a smaller version of the dining table that was covered with all the ornaments for the tree. On the wall across from the sofa was a beautiful, whitewashed brick fireplace, and above that was the very large television I had splurged on. Beside the fireplace sat my guitar and on the other side in the corner by the slider that led to the balcony was my tall tree.

"I see you still love Christmas," Ryan said pointing to the bare tree that was waiting for decorations.

"Of course, I do. Remember how I used to be around Christmas time?"

Ryan's mouth turned into a big smile, and he laughed. "How I could I forget? You made sure we were all there to decorate the tree and you would have Conor lift you up to put the topper on the tree.

Then you would make us all string the lights on the outside of the house.

When we finished and came inside, you and your dad would always be sitting on the sofa curled up with hot chocolate. I always remember walking in and see you leaning into your dad his arm wrapped around your shoulders. God, he loved his little girl."

Ryan smiled at me, and I smiled back because I used to love having that moment every year with my dad.

"Shit, Kenna, do you remember the year, I think, yes, it was the year before you left for college. Finn fell from the roof of the porch. The fucker landed in the bushes."

We both started laughing.

Okay, I can do this, I thought to myself, *I can be normal with Ryan.*

"We had so many memories together."

"That we did." He grinned.

An idea popped into my head. "Help me decorate?"

I walk over to the coffee table, avoiding the pile of lights on the floor that I had tripped on a few minutes ago.

"I don't know."

"Come on, Ryan, it will be fun." With a smile, he

proceeded to put his coffee down. "Okay, you twisted my arm—both arms."

The two of us spent the next two hours wrapping the lights around the tree, hanging ornaments, and draping shiny icicles off the branches.

"Oh, uhm, hey," Ryan said. "I think we work ourselves into a corner."

He was right, we had somehow gotten stuck between the tree and the wall while trying to wrap the garland around the tree.

With care, we placed each of the remaining ornaments on the tree, with me fixing the ones Ryan put too close together.

"Seriously?" He would roll his eyes every time I separated them. "What was wrong with that one."

"Well, for starters, you can't hang two of the same shape and color next to each other." I started to think he was doing it on purpose to drive me crazy.

When we finished, we took a step back and admired our work.

"Where is the topper?" Ryan looked around the room.

I smiled and said, "Still in the box on the island."

Ryan turned and walked over to the island. I couldn't help but watch him as he walked over. The man always had a strut that made his ass move so nicely and, in those jeans he had on, I couldn't help but stare.

When Ryan turned back with the topper in his hands, he smirked, making me think he completely caught me watching his ass.

Sue me it's a very nice butt. I thought.

He held the topper up overhead. "Let's get it on there."

I scanned the apartment for anything tall enough for me to stand on that would reach the top of the tree. "Shit. I don't have a ladder or step stool."

One glance at the swivel chairs around the dining room table, and I dismissed those.

Hell, I didn't need a broken arm or leg for Christmas.

"No need, you can climb onto my shoulders. I will hold you." He came up in front of me.

"No. No, that's okay. I will just get a ladder next time I'm out."

"Nonsense." Ryan pulled me over to the coffee table. "Get on the table. When I bend down, just climb onto my shoulders."

"I don't know."

"It's fine. Come on. Let's go."

I just stared at him for a moment and realized one thing.

Yup. He's going to make me climb onto his shoulder. Fuck.

With my legs shaking a little from nerves, I climbed onto my new coffee table. Slowly, I drew in a deep breath, then made my way onto his shoulders, preying he wasn't feeling the heat pooling between my legs.

Ryan grabbed hold of my legs, and when he felt I was secure, he grabbed the tree topper and handed it to me.

"All right?" he asked. You good up there?"

No. No, I'm not good. The words screamed inside my head.

I was sitting on his shoulders thinking how I really just want to be in another position with my legs wrapped around him.

"Yup. All good," I murmured.

After a few minutes of leaning forward, I reach up. I almost fell back a few times. Finally, I got the damn topper on top of the tree.

"Okay," I said. "It's on. You can put me down."

He swung me around, catching me in his arms.

A screech of a yelp left my lips, and I instinctively wrap my arms around his neck.

Now, here I was, facing Ryan. His arms wrapped around the back of my thighs, and my hands looped around his neck.

He slid me down his body. My toes were the first things to hit the floor, and as he lowered me, the soles of my feet pressed down. Slowly, I unwrap my hands from his neck and slid them down the front of his chest to his stomach. As soon as he was sure I had secured my footing, he let me go and stepped back.

I gazed up and meet his golden eyes. I swore they were burning into me because I felt so hot that I could feel each sweat bead building and rolling down.

Turning away, I pretended to look for something, anything, really just so I didn't have to look at him.

A ringing phone cut through the silence, and I turned back, realizing it was Ryan's cell.

"It's Conor." He held the phone out for me to see.

Ryan swiped the phone and put it on speaker. "Conor, what's up."

I walked over to have a seat on the sofa so they could talk.

"Dude, why the fuck aren't you at the gym. Where are you? They just announced the nominees for the MMA awards," Conor shouted through the phone.

"Fuck. I forgot that was today. I-I'm . . . I'm at um, Kenna's place." Ryan's voice shook.

Yep. Leave it to my brother to make Ryan shaky.

"Kenna's place? Oh, how is she?" he asked.

"How about you ask her yourself, you're on speaker."

"Hi, Micky. How are you?" Conor asked.

"Hey, Conor," I said in response. "I'm good."

"Actually, this includes you too, Kenna. So, I'm glad you're on with us," Conor said.

"Dude, tell me." Ryan was getting a little impatient.

I give him a look of confusion, trying to understand what the big deal was. I had never really paid attention to any of the fighting stuff. It just never interested me. But I had a feeling that this was a big deal in their world.

"Okay. Okay, so . . . Ry, you were nominated for 'Knockout of the Year' for your last fight!" Conor practically yelled in excitement.

"Fuck! Yes! I knew that knockout was fucking awesome," Ryan yelled back.

"I know. I know. I knew there was no way you wouldn't be nominated. The way you dropped Romeo was fucking amazing."

God. If my neighbors can hear any of this, they're gonna think two people are fighting in here by all the yelling. I exhaled a heavy sigh. *Damn. They're so stupidly-excited.*

"That's not all. Finn and I were both nominated for trainer of the year!"

"Hell, yeah! That's amazing and so deserved."

"There's more and Kenna, this includes you."

Pointing to myself as he could see me, I said, "Me . . . How? Why?"

"Well, the gym was nominated for best gym, which included you as a third owner. Listen, Mick, the awards are in Orlando. Finn and I really would like it if you attended the ceremony with us this year. You're a part of this with us. This is for dad," he said, ending with a low voice.

I looked at Ryan in disbelief. An award ceremony for a gym that I owned a third of but had no involvement in.

This is crazy.

"I don't know Conor it seems silly for me to go," I said. "I don't do anything for the gym."

"Micky, please," Conor begged. "Finn and I want you to be there."

I looked at Ryan and shrugged my shoulders, not sure how to answer.

"She'll be there," Ryan replied.

My eyes grew wide in shock that he would answer for me.

"Yes," Conor shouted with excitement. "Micky, thank you. Friday night, we celebrate. I will call

Mike over at Journey's and get us on the VIP list."
With that last statement, Conor disconnected the
line.

"Journey's?" I asked Ryan.

"It's a club in downtown Orlando. The owner
and bouncers frequently use the gym." Ryan pulled
me up from the sofa. "Fuck. Kenna, I was nominated
for fucking knockout of the year."

He wrapped his arms around me, then lifted me
off the ground. With my feet dangling, he swung me
around. I couldn't help but squeeze him back and
laugh in light of his complete joy and excitement.

As he places me back down, he grabbed my hand
in his. "Come on. Let's go do something fun to
celebrate."

15

RYAN

"What do you have in mind?" Kenna walked over to the side of the sofa and grabbed her brown boots.

I watched her slip them on. They were short boots that went to her ankle but had a little heel that made her stand just a little taller.

God, she looks so good. I thought.

All I could think about was unwrapping that green silk scarf from her neck and using it to tie her to the bed and make her scream my name in absolute pleasure.

Shaking the thought out of my head, I said, "Let's go get something to eat and grab a drink to celebrate. We can head to Jenkins. They're open now."

"Yes, that sounds great. I actually think they have someone playing this evening." Kenna stood and walked to the door. As she made her way to the door, she tripped over the left-over lights that we hadn't picked up yet.

"Fucking lights. Shit. It's like I don't know how to walk." She laughed.

I couldn't help but laugh. She was so freaking beautiful. Even when she was tripping over things.

"Don't laugh at me." She backhanded me on the chest, then shook her hand. "Oow."

Once again, I couldn't help but laugh.

Foregoing a table, we sat at the bar because Kenna wanted to be by the stage, next to the guy playing guitar and singing.

After we had celebrated with a couple of shots of tequila, we both ordered a beer and a couple of burgers with fries. A few people stopped to congratulate me on the nomination.

I look over at Kenna, sitting on a stool. She was swaying to the music playing.

Once she finished her burger, leaving only the fries and pickles to pick at, she jumped off the bar stool and stood beside me.

"Want another beer?" I asked her.

"Sure." She nodded.

"Hey." I leaned in close. "I gotta hit the head. Be right back." With my spoken words, I made my way to the restroom.

Inside, I stepped around god knows what on the

floor, then found an unused urinal. Once done, I shook, tucked, zipped, then washed my hands.

When I'm making my way back from the bathroom, I saw two guys over by Kenna. They were both checking her out.

"Hey, darling, you want a drink?" asked one of the men as he invaded her personal space. The other guy, his fuckin' wingman, leered and egged him on—fucking prick.

Oh, fuck no! Not on my watch.

I knew with everything she had gone through, and especially after seeing what my mother had experienced, I knew not to sneak up behind her. I didn't want to scare her, so I sat back on the barstool, turned to her, then wrapped my arm around her waist.

"You okay?" Slowly, I eased her between my legs.

Kenna being as short as she was still had to look up at me.

She smiled with more than just her mouth. It was as if her whole face smiled at me.

Those slimy motherfuckers quickly took notice and moved down to the other end of the bar.

It felt good holding her—natural even. So, I didn't dare move my arm. I just left it wrapped around her.

My hand fanned out across her stomach, and she

didn't make any attempt to move away. We were both playing with danger now.

We stayed attached like that for a few songs.

The only movement made was Kenna's hips swaying to the beat, and fuck it if I didn't enjoy it. Being here with Kenna in my arms, and listening to the music, felt like pure heaven.

I had dreams of this moment a million times, but this was different. It was better than I could have ever imagined.

When the guy playing finished, Kenna turned around, then took a step back.

"We should probably get going," she said.

"Okay." I nodded, feeling the loss of her body heat immediately.

I paid the bill and left an extra hundred on the bar for a tip.

Kenna's eyes widen. "Too bad I didn't have a few of you up in Boston. I could've used tips like that." She smiled, making her eyes brighten.

Guilt washed over me. Back in Boston, she had to hide money from the asshole to get home. Her words reminded me that I wasn't there to protect her.

Her hand slipped into mine.

"Stop it. I know what you're thinking," she said

with that sweet voice of hers. "Please. Let's move on from all that shit."

I couldn't stop myself from interlacing my fingers with hers. It felt natural as if it was where she belongs. Hand in hand, I led her out of Jenkins.

By the time I pulled into Kenna's parking lot, the sun was starting to set. I walked her to her apartment, not touching her this time, and I managed to stay back a few steps so that I wouldn't reach for her. After she unlocked the door and opened it, she turned to me with a smile dancing on her lips.

"Do you want to come in for a while?" she asked.

I knew I had to leave. Hell, I couldn't go back inside. God, I wanted nothing more than to enter that apartment, but I stayed back.

"I'm going to head home."

"All right. I'll see you later." Kenna didn't wait for me to say goodbye, she just closed the door.

It's probably for the best. I sighed. After all, If she had left the door open, I wouldn't have had the willpower to walk away. *Fuck. I want her.*

16

MACKENNA

Shutting my door, I press my back to the door and lift my head to the ceiling letting out a loud sigh.

What am I doing? I thought.

As I unwrapped the scarf around my neck, I threw it on the coat hook by the door, and then bent down, removing my boots. My feet kept moving to the slider that led to the balcony, knowing that was where Ryan had parked.

Tripping over the lights that were still thrown on the floor, I curse, "Fucking lights."

I open the slider door. A light breeze hit my bare neck. I walked to the railing and saw him. I saw Ryan walking to his truck. My eyes followed him as he approached the driver's side door. He put his hand in his pocket to grab his keys, then he did something

I was not expecting, he looked up directly into my eyes.

Even from so far away, I could feel the electricity running through me. Our eyes stayed locked on each other. I'm not sure how long we were looking at each, but I eventually broke the contact and looked away, but only for a moment, because I couldn't keep myself from staring at Ryan. I just could.

So, I glanced back at him and saw him mouth the word, 'fuck' and before I knew it, he turned, and ran —not walked—back to the door to my building.

Oh. My. God. He's coming back.

I spun around on the balls of my feet, and did the same thing—I ran to my door, jumping over the pile of lights this time. I ripped my door open and stepped into the hall. I could hear him before I saw him.

His footsteps slammed down on each step he took. They echoed.

Then he turned the corner, and our eyes met. He only took about two steps before I took off in a sprint.

I ran to him—I ran to him like the world was ending and he was the last person on earth, the only person. I jumped into the air toward him, knowing and trusting in him completely, because I knew that he'd catch me.

Without fail, his arms came out, and he caught me with his hands on my ass. I immediately wrapped my legs around him. He instinctively turned and pinned me against the wall.

Our mouths collided. And the moment they did, we both opened up, immediately needing each other.

I moaned his name into his mouth, and he lightly growled into mine.

The click of a latch sounded, and we both released our mouths and looked to find the source— my neighbor was peeking out into the hallway.

"Oh my," I hear the little old lady say.

I bury my head into Ryan's neck and both of us murmured, "I'm sorry, ma'am."

She shook her head, slamming her door shut.

We both started to laugh. Without letting go of me, Ryan walked us into my apartment, then kicked the door shut with his foot. As he slid his hands up my back, I removed my legs from around his waist, I slid myself down his body, feeling his erection.

When my feet hit the floor, he caged me against the wall with both hands on either side of my face.

"Kenna, I'm going to ask you once," he said. "Do you want this?"

I didn't have the breath to speak, so I nodded my head up and down.

"Kenna, I need to hear the words," Ryan whispered tenderly into my ear, and then his golden-brown eyes met mine.

"Yes," I whisper back.

That was all he needed then his mouth crashes back down onto mine. His hands were everywhere: at my neck, on my shoulders, and on my arms.

When he reached my wrists, he lifted them above me, holding me against the wall.

"Kenna, fuck, I need you. I want to savor every inch of you, but I swear, right now, I need to be inside you. Like now."

My heart was pounding so hard against his chest that I know he could feel it.

"Yes, please. Now, Ryan."

Lifting me again, he carried me to my room.

"Lights," I said as he approached the pile on the floor.

Without missing a beat, he stepped over them, into my room, and then to my bed. Leaning over me, I watched his calloused hands unbutton my jeans, and then slide my zipper down.

When his hands slid to my hips, I lift them, so he could remove my jeans. As I sit up, he grabbed my shirt, and I lift my arms in the air. In one smooth tug, he slid it over my head.

I removed the hair tie holding my hair up, and Ryan gasped when my hair fell over my shoulders. I laid back on the bed, bare except for my matching white lace panties and bra.

"God, Kenna, you are so beautiful." He gazed down at me while he was pulling his own shirt up and over his head.

I had seen Ryan without a shirt before, but with him standing over me like this, I couldn't help but gasp to myself because he was absolutely gorgeous. I sat back because I couldn't wait any longer.

My hands went to his button and I lowered his jeans as fast as I could. I removed his boxers with his jeans, taking all of him in. The small trail of hair that ran into the V, led to his erection. With his hand under my chin, he lifted my face to his.

"Kenna, I need you now. I've dreamt about this moment since I was seventeen."

As I lowered back down to the bed, I opened my legs, giving myself to him. Ryan looked at me, his eyes burning with desire. He brought a finger to my wet panties.

"Fuck, Kenna, you are so wet."

I lift my neck, closed my eyes, and moan from the feel of his finger. When I open my eyes, he had both hands on my panties, and in one clean swoop, he tore them in half.

"Ryan," I gasped. He crawled over me, kissing his

way up my stomach to my breast, and gently bit my nipple through the lace of my bra.

This time, I moaned his name, "Ryan, please."

I could feel his tip at my opening, and I wrapped my legs around him, wanting him to push inside me.

"Kenna, I promise you, I'm clean. I get tested for every fight."

I gazed at his gorgeous face, my hands running down his chest and over every muscle.

"I'm as well. I was tested not long after I came home. And I'm on the pill."

I pulled my legs a little tighter around him, inviting him in. As he entered me, we both moaned.

"Holy fuck, Kenna. You feel so good!"

At that very moment, I was home, and a tear fell out of the corner of my eye, and Ryan kissed it away.

"I'm right here, baby," he whispered. "I promise I will always be here." With that, his movements began to go faster with each thrust building up inside me.

His hand found its way in between us and began to circle my clit, and that's all it took.

Holy god, he feels so good.

I couldn't control myself. My head moved side to side, and I moaned his name.

"Oh god, Ryan, oh god," I yell.

"That's right, baby, cum with me," he said, and

that was all it took. Together, we both went over the edge. Each yelled the other's name.

He crashed down on top of me momentarily before putting all his weight on his elbow. Both of us were breathing as if we had just run twenty miles. We were covered in each other's sweat.

I felt every emotion and I broke. Tears rolled out of each eye.

Ryan grabbed my face, wiping the tears away.

"Baby, what's wrong . . . D-did I hurt you," he asked tenderly. Even his touch on my face covered concern.

"No," I cry as I look away.

"Look at me, baby," he said, pulling my face to his.

He had never used words of endearment with me. At this very moment, I felt like I was his, as much as he had always been mine. "Tell me why you are crying."

"I-I just," I couldn't get the words out because I knew he wasn't going to say them back to me, but God, I was so in love with him. I had been in love with Ryan since, well, pretty much forever. As tears flowed and my heart beat so fast, I could pass out. Ryan pushed up onto his knees and pulled me up with him.

Then he spoke, holding my face in both his

hands, so I had to look at him. He ran his thumbs along my face, wiping the tears from my cheeks, and he said, "Kenna, Baby, I love you. I love you so much, please tell me what's wrong."

My eyes went wide. "W-what did you say?" I asked, not believing he had said that to me. I must have been imagining things.

"I love you," he said again, this time almost in a whisper. "It's you, Kenna. It has always been you." I grabbed hold of Ryan's face, bringing him down to me, and kissed him softly this time. Taking my time, enjoying him, tasting him, and feeling him.

"Ryan," I said softly, "I'm so in love with you. I've loved you for so long I can't even remember when I started."

Ryan wrapped me in his arms and rolled over, so he was lying on the bed, and I was straddling him. "God, Kenna, you are so beautiful." I immediately laid my head onto his hard, muscular chest and smiled. We lay like that for a few minutes when Ryan began to speak softly. "Kenna?"

"Mmmm," was all I responded, never moving my head from his chest.

With his fingers softly rubbing up and down my back, he continued, "Baby, you have ink."

It wasn't a question. I knew he had seen the tattoo on my back between my shoulder blades. I moved my head up, facing him with my chin now on his chest."

"I do." I rolled off Ryan and onto my back with my head hitting the pillow beside him and said, "You have ink as well."

With a smirk, he responded, "Kenna, I'm covered in ink; you already know that. But I never knew you had any. Roll over; I want to see it."

I swallowed a lump that was starting to form in my throat. I wasn't sure how he would take my tattoo, but there was no hiding it now. I rolled over onto my stomach, so he would have a view of the ink on my back.

Ryan slowly moved his fingers along the musical note that was inked on my skin. He slowly traced the cursive writing for three names that formed the music note. Suddenly, I felt his hot breath by my ear.

"Baby," he whispered, "You have my name inked on your body."

"I do," was all I stated, keeping my head on the pillow.

Ryan continued tracing his name as he stated, not asking, "Tell me about your tattoo."

"After I got back to Boston from Dad's funeral, I wanted to get a tattoo in memory of my mom and my dad. I thought of the music note because, well, I'm a musician, and I always played with my mom.

Then I came up with the idea of the music note being the names of the most important people in my life, and that was Conor, Finn."

I lifted my head from the pillow and looked into Ryan's gorgeous brown eyes with golden specks.

"And you?" He leaned down and kissed my shoulder.

"The blue butterfly is for my dad, and the pink butterfly on the other side is for my mom."

Ryan spoke before I could give the reason, "Butterflies because you wrote that song with your mom."

I stared at him again in disbelief "How did you know about that?" I asked.

"I remember playing with Conor and Finn out in your backyard. You and your mom were sitting on the deck. You were both playing your guitars, and you sang the song." Ryan spoke of the memory.

Me, I just stared, shocked that he remembered.

Ryan continued to gently stroke my back, and then soon his hand went lower, and he grabbed hold of my ass. His mouth found my ear, and he licked the spot between my ear and neck, then growled.

"Fuck, baby, you are so sexy."

I know he felt the shake in my body, his hot breath giving me the chills.

He slowly brought his tongue down my neck, kissing my shoulders, working his way to his name, inked on my skin down my back, and then a nip at my ass cheek. Slowly, he brought his body back up, kissing, licking, and nipping all the way up my body.

His erection pressed against me, making me ache with need for him.

"God, you taste so good, babe," he said, but before he could kiss my mouth, my phone dinged.

I was absolutely fine with ignoring it, but then it went off again, and then a third time—that was a whole other story.

Ryan leaned over the bed and grabbed it from my pants that were piled on the floor.

"Here, baby." He handed it to me.

When I turned it over, I saw Conor's name.

> Conor: I really want to talk to you.

> Conor: We can't keep avoiding each other we need to talk about everything .

> Conor: I'm going to head over to your place.

> Be there in a few.

"Oh, shit!" I immediately pushed Ryan off me and sat up. "Fuck. Conor is on his way here."

"Oh, fuck." Ryan jumped from the bed and immediately grabbed his boxers and jeans.

"What are we going to do," I asked with panic in my voice

"Fuck, Kenna, Conor is going to fucking kill me." He turned to grab his shirt and pull it over his head almost as fast as he ripped it off earlier.

I swiped my phone, then pushed Conor's contact, and as soon as he answered, I said, "Hey, Con, I'm not home right now. I'm out. How about I meet you for a drink instead."

Ryan continued to dress but was watching me.

"Okay. I will see you there in about twenty minutes. Bye." As I hit the end button, I looked over at Ryan, then grinned. "Calm down. He isn't coming. I'm going to meet him at Thirsty's for a drink."

I made my way to the other side of the bed where Ryan was standing. Hands on his chest, I looked up at him and asked jokingly, "Aww. Is the big bad fighter afraid of my brother?"

Ryan lowered his face just inches from my mouth. "Fuck right, I'm." He wrapped his arms around my lower back, pulling me into him. His mouth claimed mine. Immediately, I opened up to him and moaned into his mouth.

Twenty minutes later, I was pulling into the parking lot of Thirsty's. I immediately saw Conor leaning against his truck, waiting for me. I pulled in a few spots down from him.

"You could have gone in and ordered a drink," I yelled to him as I unfolded myself from my car.

I should have known he would be outside waiting for me. Conor was so overly protective of me. He would never let me be in a parking lot by myself.

Conor made his way over to me, wrapping an arm around my shoulder."

"You are not walking alone through a parking lot," he said, proving what I already knew. "Especially at night."

I rolled my eyes as we entered the bar, then made my way to an empty booth. We both ordered our drinks and silently waited for them to be delivered.

Conor was fighting with himself. He was always protective over me, even more so after our dad passed away. I knew he felt he needed to take on the fatherly role; it was just who he was. Once the waitress put our drinks down and finished making sure we were all set, Conor finally spoke.

"I hate this distance between us. I hate feeling like we lied to you regarding the trust Dad had set up."

Before Conor could finish, I interrupted him because my reaction at our lunch back in October when I returned home was not fair or logical.

"Conor, stop. I'm sorry for how I reacted at lunch. When I got back, I was not in the right head-space. I was dealing with; well, you know what I was dealing with."

Conor furrowed his brows, and his jaw twitched. I could see the anger on his face over the abuse I had dealt with.

"When you and Finn told me about the trust, I just felt like there was another part of my life that I was not in control of," I said. "And that was just silly of me to think. I know you and Finn always have the best intentions and will always protect and be there for me. I shouldn't have responded that way."

I slid my hand across the table and laid it over Conor's hand.

"Let's just move on from this," I pleaded with him. "Let's leave the past where it belongs. In the past."

Conor's face softened with a smile, and he squeezed my hand, letting me know we were okay.

"I love you, Micky. I will never be okay with what

happened in Boston or with that motherfucker, but for everything else, we're good."

We stayed and finished our drinks, discussing the gym, the upcoming MMA awards, and how we would spend Christmas. We decided we would have it at the house, and we would make Christmas together as a family: me, Conor, Finn, and Ryan. I couldn't help but smile as we discussed everything.

I was finally feeling at peace being back home. I was becoming who I was before Brad took control of my life. I knew I would never be exactly who I was before Brad. I knew I would be stronger. Sitting across from Conor, I felt the love and support of my family and knew that with their help, I would become even better than I was. I would be even stronger.

Walking out of Thirsty's, I wrapped my slim arms around Conor's strong waist and leaned into him.

"I love you . . . Because of you, Finn, and Ryan, I will become stronger. I want you to know I'm all right, and I know I will be better than all right with my *deartháir* by my side."

I had used the Irish word for brother—*deartháir*.

Conor hugged me tight and said, "Love you, Micky."

He gave me a tight hug and a kiss on top of my head and then opened my car door.

"Be careful and go straight home," he said. "It is getting late."

A smile bloomed on my lips because I wasn't heading home tonight. After shutting my car door, I reached into my purse for my phone and opened a text to Finn.

> Me: Love you, deartháir.

A minute later, Finn responded.

> Finn: Love you, Micky.

Driving out of Thirsty's, I took a left to go to the one person that I felt the safest with . . . Ryan.

17

MACKENNA

Three Months Later . . .

Pulling into a parking spot in the same Toyota I'd driven back into town, my phone dinged with a text. I rummaged through my things, finally grabbing my phone to see the message from Jeff. I'd been home for six months, and nearly three months had passed since Ryan and I admitted our love for each other, all the while keeping our relationship a secret. We both agreed that it wasn't the right time to tell Conor.

Despite our good relationship, I could see that Conor still felt tormented by the abuse I'd suffered. He believed he'd failed me, and no matter how often I reassured him that wasn't the case, I could see in his eyes that he blamed himself.

I was surprised to discover that Finn already knew about Ryan's feelings for me. One night, as we lay in bed talking, the conversation turned to my brothers and how they might react to our relationship. Ryan told me about a night after a fight when he'd had too much to drink celebrating his victory. He had confided in Finn about his feelings for me, expressing that he'd missed me and had felt this way for a very long time.

Finn wasn't surprised to hear that Ryan had feelings for me, mentioning how Ryan would always stare at me or let his hugs linger a bit too long. Finn also warned Ryan that Conor might not take the news well, as he had always been the protective brother and wouldn't want his little sister involved with a fighter. Ryan and I decided it would be best to keep our relationship private for a while as we explored our feelings and determined the future of our relationship.

When I left Thirsty's that night, I drove straight to Ryan's house without a second thought. I knew he was the one I wanted to be with. I arrived wearing the clothes I'd thrown on after our first time together: a ratty old concert t-shirt tied to expose my navel, black yoga pants, sneakers, and my messy, post-coital hair in a bun. I knew I looked like a hot mess, but when Ryan opened the door and eyed me from head to toe, my body tingled.

He took a step toward me, wrapping his muscular, inked arm around my waist, pulling me against him.

"Damn, my girl is hot," he whispered into my ear, pulling me even tighter and lifting me off the step.

With a kick, he shut the door behind us and carried me straight to his bedroom and into his bed. Since then, I've spent most nights in that bed.

Life at this moment was going wonderfully. I spent each day writing music and performing at local spots several nights a week. Ryan was in full training mode for his next fight scheduled in September.

Despite training late into the evenings, he always managed to come to watch me perform. Conor, Finn, Chrissy, and Ryan all showed their support. I could tell that our secret relationship was starting to weigh on Ryan. He had mentioned a few times how much he hated keeping it a secret from his best friend. Moreover, Conor and Finn were Ryan's trainers, so trust was crucial.

I knew Ryan wanted to come clean, but I didn't want Conor to freak out. I thought if we gave it a little more time when we did tell him, he'd see that we were absolutely committed to each other, and there was no risk of me getting hurt or heartbroken.

Now here I was sitting in the parking lot of one of the many hotels located in Orlando. That night, I was performing at the swanky bar off the lobby. I had been told when they booked me for that night to expect a good crowd due to a real estate convention being held there. So I decided to step it up and went with a sexier outfit than my typical laid-back look.

Before heading out, Ryan had stopped by my place, and his eyes nearly popped out of his head when he saw me.

"Wow, baby, you looked so fucking good! Turn and show me that pretty ass of yours," he said, grabbing my hand and twirling me around so he could get a full view.

He pushed into my backside, and I could already feel his growing erection against my tight black Capri pants. With some extra height from my cute black ankle boots with a three-inch heel, Ryan's mouth came to my bare shoulder, and he licked all the way up the exposed skin of my neck.

I had worn my hair pulled back over my left shoulder. Before letting go of me, he trailed his fingers over his name on the music note inked between my shoulder blades—he had an unobstructed view of my whole back thanks to the open back halter top I was wearing.

"God, Kenna, you are so beautiful."

My heart melted every time he said how beautiful he thought I looked.

"Hey," he said. "Is Chrissy going tonight?"

I turned and wrapped my arms around him because, well, let's face it was impossible to keep my hands off his gorgeous hard body. "Not tonight she is working on some new big marketing campaign for a brewery that's opening a few towns over. Why?" I asked.

Ryan slowly moved me back into my apartment, giving me his beautiful golden eyes. I knew he was about to tell me something that bothered him because his eyes always told me how he felt.

"Conor and Finn have me back at the gym tonight to train. September will come quickly and the guy I'm fighting, Flint is young and up and coming. They want me to do extra training, so I'm ready. This means I can't come tonight, nor can Conor or Finn."

I seriously have the best guy. "I'm fine. I don't need a babysitter, Ryan. I can take care of myself."

"I don't like you leaving alone," he said. "Your performances end pretty late. I'll come when I'm done, so you are not walking to your car all by yourself."

"Ryan, stop. You're going to be exhausted. Go home and sleep after training. I will be fine. I'm sure I can get the manager to walk me to my car. I promise everything will be fine." I placed both hands on his face and rubbed my thumb over his jaw, putting him at ease.

"Promise me you won't walk out alone," Ryan said in earnest.

I simply replied, "I promise."

18

MACKENNA

Later, as I was leaving my apartment to head to the hotel, I received a text and smiled when I saw it was from Jeff. I hadn't seen him for months. I owed him so much for everything he did for me back in Boston. He didn't have to help me, but he did, and because of that, he'd become more than just a friend—like another brother to me. When he texted last night to say he was moving to Fort Lauderdale for a bartending job so he could be near the beach and focus on writing a book, I was beyond excited.

Although there would still be some distance, three hours was nothing compared to traveling to Boston. I had time before I needed to set up for my performance, so I took the opportunity to text Jeff. He told me that Brad still visited the bar, not as frequently as when I first left, but every couple of weeks.

Jeff said Brad was furious, making comments about how I couldn't leave him and that he'd make sure he got me back. It was an unsettling feeling, but I reminded myself I was far away from him and had no intention of returning.

Glancing at my phone, I noticed the time, so I texted Jeff.

> Me: Got to head in.
>
> Me: I'm performing tonight.
>
> ME: Keep me posted on the move.

Jeff replied almost immediately.

Jeff: Will do.

Jeff: Can't wait to see you soon!

With that, I tossed my phone in my purse, grabbed my guitar, and exited the car to head into the hotel. As I made my way to the bar area, the manager met me and showed me to the stage and where I could set up. The mic and speakers were already in place, so I just needed to make sure my guitar was tuned and ready to go.

As I worked on my guitar, I felt a sickening sensation in my gut, so I headed to the bar to ask for some water. I recognized the bartender, Jessica, from a few other times I'd performed here. She was a friendly college girl from Tennessee. We made small talk, and I mentioned how I felt like I was being watched.

"Of course, you're being watched," she responded reassuringly. "For one, you're incredibly attractive, and you're a performer, so yes, you'll be watched!"

I shrugged. "You're right about the performing, not so much the attractive part!" I downed the rest of my water, and Jessica refilled it for me to take with me on the stage.

Slinging my guitar over my shoulder and adjusting the mic to the right height I took a breath to calm my nerves. It was strange to have nerves. I've not been nervous to perform since I was a teen. Halfway through my set, my nerves started to settle, I fed off the crowd and had a great performance.

When I finished the last song, "Fight Song" by Rachel Platten—I wasn't sure why I ended with that song, but it felt appropriate tonight—I thanked everyone for coming out and wished them a good night.

Methodically, I began to pack up my guitar and peeked at my phone to see a missed text from Ryan.

> Ryan: Text me when you're headed home.

> Ryan: Then text me when you get
> home.

> Ryan: I'm done training and just icing
> my knee.

Hmm, icing his knee. I wonder what happened.

> Me: Just finished packing up and
> going to head out.

> Me: What happened to your knee?

It was only seconds before Ryan replied.

> Ryan: Con was in a shit mood.

> Ryan: He had me in a leg submission
> and held it too long.

> Ryan: Fucking asshole!

With that, I threw my phone back in my purse
and had the manager walk me to my car. I was home
in no time exhausted and looking forward to dropping into my bed and falling asleep. As soon as I
entered my apartment, I whipped my shoes off and
threw them to the side of the sofa, and made my way
to my room to change and wash up. I figured I
would text Ryan once I got into bed maybe even call
him to wish him good night.

As I was washing my face to remove the little makeup, I had on I heard a faint knock on my door. I smiled immediately.

Ryan is here!

I quickly wiped my face with a hand towel throwing it on the vanity as I turned with a hop skip and jump to answer the door.

I opened the door quickly ready to throw myself into Ryan's arms. As soon as the door opened, and I saw the person standing on the other side, I quickly grabbed at the handle to shut the door. But before I could, I was shoved inside.

"Did you really think you could leave me?" Brad growled in anger.

I tried to get by him and out the door, but Brad grabbed hold of my arms and pulled me back.

"Where do you think you're going?" he growled once more.

He held one of my arms tight, and he used his other hand to slam the door shut and lock it.

I swallowed the rising bile and seethed. "How did you know where I was?"

Looking into his evil angry eyes, I started to put it together. Feeling watched at my performance and then I remembered there was a Real Estate convention being held there.

I stared, unblinking. "You were at the hotel . . . You followed me home!"

It wasn't a question because I already knew it was true.

Brad didn't say anything for a moment, then as he pulled me further into my apartment, he slammed me hard against the wall. So hard, the back of my head hit the wall from the force. It took a minute for me to shake out the stars that I was seeing.

Fear was starting to take over me, but I did my best to maintain eye contact and show Brad no fear. Still holding my arms pushed against the wall, he leaned into my face.

"Did you actually think you could just walk out and leave me?" he spoke in the angriest tone I'd ever heard come out of his mouth.

I stayed silent but maintained eye contact.

His hands squeezed my arms tighter, almost bringing tears to my eyes.

"Answer me," he whispered inches from my face, his tone icy.

I'd seen Brad angry and violent before, but the anger he had now was utterly terrifying. Even though he frightened me, I was determined to fight. Too many times in the past, I had coward in fear, but not this time.

"Fuck you," I snapped back, practically spitting

the words in his face.

My head slammed into the wall once more, this time from the force of the punch that hit me in my face. Immediately, a wave of dizziness washed over me, followed by a sharp tingling pain right below my eye.

A liquidy warmth ran down my cheek—blood.

"Fuck you." I wasn't sure what had come over me, but again, I practically spit in his face "Did you hear me, fuck you!"

Once again, my head bounced off the wall, and a burning sensation formed on my lips.

After the second hit, the dizziness was too extreme. My legs could barely hold me up. If Brad's body hadn't pinned me against the wall, I surely would've fallen to the floor.

Brads hands move to my throat holding me tight but not squeezing.

This time, he followed my eyes as I tried to look away.

"Look at me, Kenna." A nauseating pause hung in the air. "This is what's going to happen. You're going to pack your bag, and you are coming back with me . . . Do you understand?"

I was still dizzy from smacking my head against the wall. It was hard to focus, but I knew I had to get away.

This won't end well. The thought brought goose-pimpled flesh to the surface of my arms.

With Brad's hand around my throat, he was no longer holding my arms, so I gathered up all my strength, then brought my hands up. With fury I didn't realize I possessed, I dug my fingernails into his face as hard as I possibly could and dragged them right down his cheeks, opening fissures in his skin as I went.

"What the fuck?" He immediately backed up.

Taking the small window of opportunity given, I lifted my leg as fast and as hard as I could, landing my knee right between his legs. When he bent over in pain, I took advantage of that moment to try and get away.

I turned and ran through my bedroom door. But before I could get the door all the way closed and locked, Brad kicked it in, sending me crashing to the floor from the impact. I scurried back using my feet and hands, but before I could get to my feet, Brad was standing over me.

Time ticked by so fast that before I knew what had happened, he kicked me in the ribs.

Pain radiated up and around my torso, taking my breath away. I turned away from him, moaning in pain. Knowing the worst was yet to come, I gave him my back and curled into a ball with my arms over my head—trying to make as small of a target as possible.

Once again, he proceeded to kick me. The impact was solid and followed by three more.

The pain was excruciating, but I knew I couldn't give up. I had to fight.

"Come here." Brad grabbed a hold of my hair and yanked me up and pushed me onto the bed.

"No. Please." I screamed out in pain. It took all my strength to move to the other side of the bed, then get to my feet.

The pain was unbearable, making it hard to fill my lungs. Dizziness made my movements slow and sluggish, made it hard to get away from his approach.

"Where do you think you're going?" Brad flipped me onto my back, slamming on top of the bed.

Climbing over me, he straddled my hips. He leaned forward, holding my arms down.

"Do you really think you could get away from me?" he spoke in a voice that I had never heard from him. The voice was so angry.

I knew if I didn't continue to try and get away, I wouldn't make it out of my apartment alive, so I struggled to get out of his grip.

"You're fucking leaving this apartment either with me or in a body bag."

My eyes opened wide, looking directly into his. I saw then the absolute evil in him. I turned my face away, trying to find anything that I could use to help me escape.

As my eyes quickly scanned the room, the scissors on my end table—the ones that I used to cut the tags off my pants—would give me a fighting chance.

All I needed to do was get out from under Brad, then get to the end table. At that moment, I stopped struggling.

"I will go with you," I stated softly.

Brad instantly loosened his grip but didn't remove himself from me. Instead, he kept my body pinned to the bed with his. Brad lowered his face to mine. Now, only inches from me, his breath blew over my face.

"That's my girl," he calmly whispered, and then he kissed me.

Brad kissed me hard enough to make me cry out, and the minute my lips parted in a sob, his tongue forced its way into my mouth.

The coppery taste of hit my tastebuds, and my lips ached from the brutal transgression. He loosened his grip, then pawed at my breasts.

If I can get him off me, I thought to myself, *I can get to the end table and grab the scissors.*

I knew I needed to make a move, and fast.

Slowly, Brad ended the kiss, which was my cue to make my move.

With my mouth still partially parted, I leaned into him as if to kiss him, then bit into his bottom lip as hard as I could. Hard enough to tear through the thin tissue.

When he instinctively tried to move away, I used all the strength I had and brought my fist to his face. Then just like I'd seen Conor do in the ring, I did it again and again. After the third punch, I was able to push him off me and roll off the bed.

Quickly, I jumped off the bed, not even feeling the pain from my injuries.

The scissors. I gotta get the scissors. I chanted over and over again in my head.

I got a hold of the scissors at the same time Brad wrapped his arms around my legs.

Raising my arms over my head, I lifted the scissors, then plunged the sharp end into one of his arms.

"You fuckin' bitch," he yelled.

He immediately let go of me and grabbed his arm in pain.

When I sprinted forward to get past him, he grabbed my leg again, and I dropped to the floor. Holding my leg tight, he spat blood out of his mouth.

"You stupid, fucking bitch." He yanked my leg back, pulling me to him.

Without thinking, I turned with the scissors still in my hand and stabbed him again. This time, hitting his shoulder. But I didn't stop there. No, I pulled the scissors back again and stabbed him once more.

Brad fell back, letting go of me.

Not wasting any time, I jumped to my feet. Cradling my ribs, I ran into the bathroom and locked the door. As soon as the door locked into place, I fell to the tiled floor and gripped the scissors tightly, waiting.

I knew I injured Brad, but I wasn't sure how badly.

"Open the fuckin' door." He banged on the door.

The jolting boom made me jump. I slid across the floor, putting as much distance as I could between the entry point and where I now sat with my back pressed against the toilet.

"Open this door," he continued to bang and yell for what felt like forever, but in reality, it was only minutes, then it was silent.

The silence scared me more than the banging because I didn't know what the hell he would do next, and then, that's when I heard a voice—the one that made my heart melt . . . Ryan's.

19

RYAN

Lying in my bed, staring at the ceiling, I wait for Kenna to text me that she was home and safe. I wondered what was taking so long. It's been an hour since she texted me that she was leaving the venue.

I bet she forgot and went to bed.

"Forget it," I mumbled, then rolled over and off the bed. I didn't even want to sleep without her next to me.

I grabbed a pair of jeans and a t-shirt tossed over a chair next to the window. I limped over to the door—thanks to Conor, the asshole—then gingerly slipping on a pair of black boots. After grabbing my wallet and keys, I left my house and made my way to Kenna's place.

She lived only about ten minutes away. So, I arrived in no time and pulled into the parking lot.

Her car sat parked in her spot.

Well, at least she made it home. Frustrated, I shook my head. She could've called or messaged.

After removing my keys and exiting my truck, I made my way to the stairs to her apartment. When I turned the corner, I noticed a few drips of what appeared to be blood on the floor. I didn't think too much of it until I got closer to her door and saw it was open.

Before I could run inside, the neighbor opened her door and peeked her head out, her eyes wild with fight.

"Get back inside." I motioned for her to stay in her place. "Lock the door and call 911."

I turned and quickly entered Kenna's apartment, seeing more blood on the floor. My heart started pounding in my chest.

As I made my way through the apartment, I followed the blood trail to her bedroom. I scanned the trashed room—blood on her bed, the blankets a mess, and things scattered on the floor. My eyes went right to the closed bathroom door. Grabbing the doorknob, I twisted it, but it was locked.

"Kenna!" After no immediate response, I yelled again, "Kenna, baby, are you in there?"

Just as I was about to kick the door in, I heard something as soft as a whisper.

"Ryan." It sounded again, but this time, it was her. "Ryan, is that you?"

"Yes, baby, I'm here. Open the door."

A few seconds later, the door opened, and I saw her—beaten and battered, with blood all over her. She fell into my arms, and I immediately wrapped my arms around her.

"Baby, what happened?" I asked. "Are you all right?"

Sirens blared. They were loud enough for me to know the police had arrived.

"It's okay, baby. It's over." I lowered us to the floor.

"I fought back," she cried into my chest.

I gently grabbed her face and lifted it up to mine.

"I fought back, Ryan. Where is he?" Fear crept into her words.

"Where is who?" I asked. "Who did this to you?"

"Brad. Brad was here, but I fought back. I stabbed him with the scissors. Where is he?" She asked, tears running down her face.

"Brad was here?" I growled out the words.

A police officer entered the room. "Let her go," the uniformed man shouted. "Step away and put your hands in the air."

"No." Kenna grabbed hold of me tighter. "He didn't do anything! It was Brad. Where is he? I stabbed him!" She continued, yelling louder, "Where is he?"

I glanced down at Kenna. "He isn't here."

Kenna dropped her face to my chest, crying, "No, no, no."

One of the policemen approached us, kneeling in front of Kenna. "Ma'am, there's an ambulance on the way. Can you tell me what happened here?"

I held Kenna as she told the police what had happened. When she finished telling them the horrid details, one of the first responders approached her. I took that opportunity to make my way over to one of the officers, Griffin Barnes, whom I recognized from the gym.

I leaned in close so no one could hear me. "Griff, you better find this *motherfucker* before her brothers, or I do."

"Ryan, right now, I'm Officer Barnes, not Barney from the gym, and you really shouldn't be saying this to me," he replied.

"I don't give a flying *fuck* who you are right now. Look at her. I will *fucking* kill him if I find him first," I seethed, making my anger known.

"I will do everything I can, but right now, you need to be with her. She needs you. Did you call Conor and Finn?" he asked.

I gave a knowing look to Griff, *fucking* Officer

Barnes, and turned to return to Kenna. As I approached, an EMS guy wheeled a stretcher inside.

Kneeling next to Kenna, I gave her a kiss on top of her head. "Let's get you to the hospital, and then I'll call Conor and Finn," I said softly.

Her big green eyes filled with tears. "Okay." She lifted her beautiful face and met my gaze.

Not long after we had arrived at the hospital, a doctor came in to examine Kenna, then sent her for a CT scan and some X-rays to check for a concussion and broken ribs.

I took that moment to gather my thoughts and called Conor and Finn. Since Conor and Finn lived in the same house, I figured it would be best if I called Finn since he was the calmer of the two—plus, he already knew how I felt about Kenna.

It wasn't lost on me that Conor would freak out when he learned about my relationship with his sister.

As I pulled up Finn's contact information, I worked to control my emotions. I took a few deep breaths, then made the call.

Finn answered almost immediately. "What the *fuck*, Ryan? Why could you possibly be calling me this late? Dude, you better not be calling me at this hour to bitch about your knee."

"Naw, just listen." I proceeded to tell him what

happened with Kenna. There was rustling in the background, and then the next thing I heard was him yelling, "Conor, wake the *fuck* up! We need to go. It's Kenna."

Silence hit the line and for a moment, I held my breath.

"I don't *fucking* know all the details," Finn said. "Ryan is at the hospital with her now. Let's go." Another quiet pause hit the line. "Ry, we're on our way," was all he said, then the call disconnected.

It wasn't long before a loud commotion hit the hallway. I knew right away it was Conor and Finn. I was in the room that Kenna was in before they took her for her X-rays and CT scan. I had just lowered my head into my hands, my elbows on my knees, trying to take everything in when I heard them.

Conor yelling at someone, demanding to know where his sister was.

"Damn." I exhaled the breath I didn't even know I was holding.

Rising to my feet, I walked out of the room to find Conor and Finn, whom I found at one of the nurse's stations.

"Conor. Finn!" I called out to them. "Over here." I stepped out of the doorway, so they could see me. "They took her for a scan and x-ray."

Walking past me, he entered the room, then turned to face me. "What the *fuck* happened, Ry?"

Conor paced the room while I told him everything I knew.

I described the trail of blood, her trashed bedroom, and how I had found her locked in the bathroom. Before I could finish, a nurse brought Kenna back into the room.

Both Conor and Finn ran to their little sister. They were visibly upset but tried to reel it in for Kenna's sake.

Finn grabbed hold of Kenna's hand, and Conor leaned in and put a hand on Kenna's injured face.

Kenna was the first to break the silence. "I'm all right." A tear ran down her cheek.

Conor wiped it away with his thumb. "Who did this to you, Micky?"

"It was Brad." Another tear escaped. "But Conor, I fought back. I fought hard. He's injured. He's injured badly. I know he is."

Before Conor could respond, there was a soft knock on the wall.

We all turned to find Officer Griff Barnes at the door.

Conor stood tall and faced Griff. "You better be here to tell me you have that fucker in custody."

Griff ignored Conor and entered the room, directing all his attention on Kenna.

"How are you feeling?" Griff asked her.

But before she could respond, Conor, whose anger was now visible to everyone in the room, answered for her, "How the fuck do you think she's feeling? Look at her."

The room stayed quiet for a moment, Griff not answering Conor. He took a few more steps toward Kenna, making me stiffen and move with him. After looking over at me for a few seconds, his attention returned to Kenna.

"If I show you a picture," he asked. "Would you be able to confirm if this is the person you say attacked you tonight?"

Kenna's eyes went wide. "Yes." She nodded.

Griff pulled a phone out of his pocket, and once he got the picture he wanted, he turned it toward Kenna.

"Is this the man?" he asked her.

"Yes. That's Brad." Her voice trembled. "You got him." It wasn't a question; it was a statement.

"A man came in for injuries not long after you arrived. He claims he received the so-called injuries when he was jumped outside his hotel," Griff stated.

"He's fucking here?" Conor and I roared at the same time.

Conor immediately headed to the door. "Where the fuck is he?"

Griff grabbed Conor, but before he could say anything else, Conor had turned and pushed Officer Griff against the wall.

"You don't want to do that." Griff held Conor's gaze. "Not when I have the uniform on."

Finn immediately ran and grabbed hold of Conor.

As Finn tried to get Conor under control, Griff moved across the room, directing his attention to Conor first.

"Look, Conor, you're a good guy. I've known you a long time, but don't think for a second I won't cuff you and bring you in for assaulting a police officer." Griff let out a heavy sigh. "Now, get your shit under control. You're not helping the situation." Then he turned to Kenna. "We will be arresting Brad. I have an officer with him. I will need an official statement, but for now, try and get some rest. I'll reach out tomorrow."

When Griff reached the door, he turned to Finn, who still had Conor held against the wall. "Keep him in check, Finn."

Finn lifted his chin in response, and then Griff was out the door.

"Fucking bury that motherfucker," Conor yelled. "Or I will!"

Finn slammed Conor against the wall once more. "Calm the fuck down, asshole! You getting' yourself arrested won't help anything. So, go sit the fuck down and shut your mouth for five minutes."

After a few minutes of us all trying to calm ourselves down and take a breather, one of the doctors walked in.

"I have some good news for you all." The doctor wrapped his stethoscope around his shoulders. "There's no concussion and no broken ribs. But you do have severely bruised ribs, as well as a sizable lump on your head," he said to her. "Not to mention the facial cuts and bruises. Tomorrow and over the next few days, I expect you'll see more discoloration."

"So, she's going to be okay?" Conor asked.

"Yes, with nothing broken, we feel comfortable discharging her," the doctor said. "One of the nurses will be by soon with all the discharge paperwork."

"Thank you, doc." Finn let out a breath of relief. "We appreciate it."

We were all thankful to hear that she had nothing broken and that she could get out of there soon. But I had no intention of letting her go anyplace but my home.

"Micky, why don't I go by your place and grab some stuff," Finn stated. "And you can head back to the house with Conor?"

"She isn't going anywhere but my house," I stated firmly, looking at both Conor and Finn. I knew there was no hiding our relationship any longer, but who gave a fuck at this point?

Conor raised an eyebrow and glared at me with anger in his eyes. "Why the fuck would she go to your house, Ry? Especially when she can come home to her own room."

It took another minute for the dots to connect for Conor, but there was no mistaking the moment he put it all together.

"Oh, hell no, Ryan." Conor's face turned a deep shade of angry red. "That isn't fucking happening."

"Come on. Back off." Finn stood next to Conor and placed a hand on his shoulder, trying to calm him down because we could all see he was about to blow.

"What the fuck is going on?" Conor asked. "Are you fucking my sister, asshole?"

"Wow, dude." Not appreciating his tone, I rose from the seat beside Kenna.

"Don't." Kenna grabbed my arm to keep me put.

Conor's eyes bouncing from Kenna's hand on my arm to my face.

"Motherfucker!" Conor roared, then he did exactly what I thought he would do—he lunged at me and got a clear shot to my face.

I stood tall, taking the punch, then placed a hand on Kenna, letting her know it was all right. Before I could say anything, Finn grabbed a hold of Conor, who was squaring up to hit me a second time.

Conor was now starting to draw the attention of some nurses.

"Back the fuck away from my sister!" he snapped at me. "I don't know what's going on here, but it better not be what I'm thinking."

Finn yanked Conor back some more, uttering words only they could hear.

Conor snapped some more, but this time in Finn's direction. "How the fuck are you okay with this? This is fucking bullshit. Ryan, you know this isn't okay. This isn't acceptable." Now looking at his sister, he calmed his voice and went on, "Micky, you know this isn't happening ever. You're coming home with Finn and me. Understand?"

Kenna, who was still holding my arm with her bruises and tears in her eyes, turned her full attention to her brother.

"No." She spoke one simple word, but it held so much authority.

My girl was holding her ground. She wasn't

going to allow her brother to dictate what she could and couldn't do.

Before I could even get a word out, Finn jumped in again, still holding Conor's arms. "Conor, we're going to leave here right now and go get Micky what she needs. We'll deal with the rest some another time. This isn't the place and definitely not the time." Looking over at me and Kenna with a lift of his chin, he said, "Micky, we'll drop by Ryan's with some of your stuff. Is there anything you can think of that you need?"

My eyes never left Conor's.

"Finn, just grab anything," she said. "I'll make do with whatever until I can go back."

"You're not going back there," Conor and I said simultaneously.

"At least you two can agree on something." Finn chuckled. "Shit, let's go, Conor, now."

Conor yanked his arm away from Finn and turned to exit the door. He looked over his shoulder.

"I'm putting an end to all of this shit," Conor said, then he was gone.

Finn lifted his sympathetic gaze to us both. "I got him, Ry. You take care of Kenna, and we'll be at your place as soon as we can."

With that, he left quickly to catch up with Conor.

We all knew Conor wasn't in a good place and would most likely do something he shouldn't.

With Conor and Finn gone, I redirected my attention to the one who needed it the most. I turned to Kenna and placed a hand on her cheek.

"Are you okay, Baby?"

Kenna leaned into my hand, grabbed my other hand, and pulled me down to her. I was now only inches from her face. She touched my cheek.

"I love you, Ryan," she whispered.

That's all it took. I brought my lips softly to hers, trying to avoid the injured side. The kiss was short and soft. When I pulled away, I gazed into her eyes.

"I love you too, Baby."

Kenna leaned forward, lightly pressing her forehead to mine. The uninjured side of her mouth lifted into a smile, then as fast as it appeared, the smile was gone, replaced by a deep-seated look of anger, fear, and determination.

"I fought back." Her voice cracked. "He was going to kill me, Ryan."

"You're safe now." I kissed the top of her head and hugged her.

"I had never been so terrified," she said. "But I knew I had to do something. I fought for my life, and I won."

The tears forming in the corners of her eyes glistened.

Gently, I wiped them away and stared at her for a few moments, gathering myself because I was so close to breaking.

"Baby." I finally found my voice. It was low and hoarse. "I can't imagine what that must have been like. I will forever be sorry I wasn't there. I promise I will never let you be alone again. I don't know what I would've done."

Kenna wiped the tears that were coming from my eyes.

"Ryan, it's okay. I'm here, I'm right here. I'm not going anywhere."

With that, we both just held on to each other. I'm not sure how much time passed before a nurse stepped into the room.

"Hi, Mackenna," the nurse cleared her throat. "I have your discharge paperwork."

20

CONOR

"I need to fuckin' punch something," I grumbled under my breath.

I had never felt such anger in my life. Twice I'd seen my sister beaten, and it was two times too many. My hands shook with the urge to kill the man responsible. I knew he had been arrested and was somewhere in the same hospital. He was lucky to be in custody, or nothing could have stopped me from ending him.

As I exited the hospital and headed to my truck, I heard my brother's voice coming up behind me.

"Conor, stop for a minute." Finn grabbed my arm. The same one he had held in my sister's hospital room. Granted, I had punched my best friend in the face upon learning he was sleeping with my sister.

This night can't get any worse.

I yanked my arm back and kept moving. I really needed to hit something or someone, but I didn't want it to be my brother.

Finn followed me, and when we reached the truck, he walked in front of me. Before I knew it, he swiped the keys out of my hands.

"What the fuck, Finn? Give me the keys. I'm not in the mood for your bullshit right now."

Without missing a beat, Finn snapped back at me, "Get in the fucking truck, Conor. We're going to Micky's. We'll get what she needs, and then we're going to Ryan's. Stop with the bullshit."

Angry and unable to deal with Finn, I turned, made my way to the passenger's side of the truck, got in, and slammed the door. We didn't speak a word on the way there. I sat, fuming with rage, trying to calm myself down. Before I knew it, we were pulling into the parking lot of my sister's apartment.

Any calmness I had gained from the ride evaporated the moment I saw the dried blood on the hallway floor. It was a stark reminder of how bad things had gotten for Micky. Finn and I continued walking, neither one of us saying a word.

When we reached the apartment, there were still a couple of police officers there. We explained who we were, and honestly, they knew us. Many officers trained at our gym. One of the officers, a woman, recognized us and stepped forward.

"Hey, guys," she said, her eyes filled with sympathy. "I know you're here to get some stuff for Micky. I'll let you in."

As we followed her, she looked back at Finn and flashed a brief, supportive smile. We mentally prepared ourselves for what we were about to see. It wasn't until we reached the bedroom that I started losing my shit again.

"I'm going to fucking kill this guy, Finn." I glared over at Finn and saw the same look I knew I had.

Finn's hands ball up into a fist so tight his knuckles turned white. Without a word, my brother turned away and walked out. That's when I knew for a fact that he understood the growing rage I now felt. Deciding it was best to give Finn a minute, I moved through my sister's bedroom.

I grabbed her suitcase from the closet and reached up for a few sweatshirts and t-shirts she had on the shelves. I didn't think she would need any jeans, so I left the closet and moved to her dresser. Next, I grabbed some sweats from one of the drawers.

As much as I didn't want to grab any of my sister's undergarments, I knew she needed them. I opened the top right drawer, reached in, and grabbed a handful, hoping I got what was needed and enough of them. I threw everything into the suitcase and made my way to the bathroom for her toiletries, grabbing everything I thought she needed. I would just go to the store if I missed anything. I needed to get the hell out of here. Seeing the blood, my sister's blood, in the bathroom was making me sick.

When I entered the living room with the suitcase, I didn't see Finn, but Pete, an officer I knew, approached.

"He stepped out," Pete said. "Needed some air."

"Can't blame him," I muttered. "Thanks. I'll go find him."

I left my sister's apartment filled with more rage than I had ever experienced in my life.

As I made my way to my truck, I kept thinking about how I had failed my sister. I should have made her move home. If she were home, that asshole never would've been able to get to her.

When I reached my truck, Finn was leaning with his forearms on the bed with his head resting on them.

"Finn," I called once I got close.

"Yeah." Finn raised his head and faced me. "Here."

He tossed me the keys, and I caught them one-handed, pulling them out of the air.

His eyes were bloodshot. I knew he had been crying.

"We'll get the asshole. He'll feel the same pain. I'll make sure of it," I stated firmly.

My brother just lifted his chin, letting me know he agreed. He turned away from me, then climbed into the truck without saying a word.

Slowly, I pulled out of the apartment complex and eased onto the street.

"They should be at Ry's by now." He gazed out the window.

I instantly gripped the steering wheel harder. Finn must have noticed because he sighed.

"Conor, Ryan loves her," he said. "He has loved her for years. Probably since we were kids."

This was too much. I couldn't handle this right now. Not only were we dealing with some asshole who thought beating women was okay, but now I had to deal with my best friend being with my sister.

No! Just no fucking way.

I raised my eyebrows and quickly glanced at Finn, who was watching for my response.

"How long have you known?" I asked my brother.

Finn went on, telling me how he wasn't aware they were officially together, but that Ryan had confessed his feelings for Kenna after a fight one night.

"That's bullshit," I said. "How the fuck—"

"Come on, Conor, how could you not know? Haven't you ever noticed the way they look at each other? Remember when we were kids, and we would be playing outside while Kenna and Mom would be sitting outside with their guitar, making up songs? Ryan would always stop and watch them. You can't tell me you never noticed that."

"Shit," I mumbled in a whisper.

Finn was right. Every time Kenna entered a room, Ryan's eyes went right to her and never left. Ryan was always the first to run over to Kenna if she fell. He was the one who always threatened any boy who tried to make contact with Kenna in high school.

"Shit. Shit. Shit!" I said each word louder than the last.

Finn smirked in the passenger seat.

"Why the fuck didn't you bring this to my attention before?"

My brother just laughed—not a small chuckle either, but a full-blown one.

"What's so funny?" I glared at him.

"You're so stupid, Conor." He just shook his head. "It was right in front of your face the whole time."

I didn't respond. Hell, what could I say to that? *Absofuckinglutely nothing!*

For the rest of the drive, I tried to get my emotions under control. As I pulled into Ryan's driveway, I was slightly calmer. But I knew the moment I entered Ryan's house, it was all going to come back. I don't know how I'm going to look at my sister and not wanna kill my best friend.

21

MACKENNA

The medical personnel behind the nurses' desk glanced my way. I was acutely aware of their eyes watching Ryan and I walk down the hallway toward the elevators. Even the nurse walking me out stole glances from time to time, making me feel like a freak on display.

Doctors walked by and studied me, then gave Ryan a judgmental stare, and other medical professionals looked up from their stations to gawk at the monstrosity that my face had become—all swollen with cuts and scratches and violent shades of black, blue, and purple. Even the people waiting to be seen all stared.

It was obvious they thought about me—about Ryan. Here I was, walking out with a large, muscular man who had his arm gently wrapped around my waist. Disgust showed on all of their faces. They assumed he was the man who had done this to me. I had to shake my head at their reactions. I wanted to scream at them, tell them he'd never hurt me and that the asshole who did would soon find himself behind bars, or so I hoped. But I remained quiet, soaking up the strength I found in Ryan's embrace.

This man holding might be strong, but he was the gentlest person I had ever known. All Ryan had ever done was love and protect me, but they didn't know that.

Once outside, he walked me to Finn's truck, which was parked in the pickup location.

"Why are we taking Finn's truck?"

With all the chaos that took place in the hospital, I must have missed something. Ryan opened the passenger door and gently helped me in. Once I was seated, he reached for the seatbelt and fastened it for me.

"Finn texted me earlier that he had put his keys in the glove box." He opened the compartment, and then pulled out the keys. "He knew I had ridden in the ambulance with you and wanted to make sure I could get you back. I'll have Finn help me get my truck tomorrow sometime."

"Oh, makes sense."

"You okay?"

"Yeah." I nodded.

The locked the door, shut it, and then made his way around to the driver's side.

As we drove back to Ryan's in silence, I tried to gather my thoughts and figured he was doing the same thing.

Ryan reached over the center console and took my hand in his. He rubbed his thumb over my bloodied knuckles.

Soft laughter escaped from between my lips.

"What?"

"Nothing." I shook my head. "It's just that usually, your knuckles are red and scraped from fighting, but now, mine are." He kissed my kissed the tender flesh, careful to not hurt me.

While Ryan drove, I laid my head against the headrest and watched as we passed the sign for the happiest place on earth. I thought about everything that had happened.

As angry as I was, trying to wrap my head around what had happened in my apartment, only added to the confusion, anguish, and anger. Also, I couldn't help but wonder what would happen now that Conor knew about Ryan and me.

Before I knew it, Ryan was pulling into his driveway and shutting off the ignition of Finn's truck. He turned to face me, never letting go of my hand. With a tenderness that was almost my undo-ing, he brought his free hand up to my cheek.

I leaned into it, needing the warmth.

"Kenna, baby, what are you thinking? Talk to me," he pleaded.

I reached up to his hand that was gently resting against my cheek. I stared at him for a moment, taking in his beautiful face that was looking at me with love.

I smiled because, honestly, how could I not smile with him looking at me like that?

"I'm afraid of what Conor is going to do," I said. "You saw him at the hospital. He isn't happy about any of this. But learning about you and me, I'm afraid he's going to freak out."

Ryan's hand left mine, making me instantly feeling the loss of his warmth. But I didn't have to feel that way for long because he brought it up to the other side of my cheek. With his hands cupping my face, he leaned forward, then gave me the softest kiss.

"Baby, don't worry about Conor," he whispered into my mouth. "I'll take care of it."

In truth, I had no words, so I pressed my lips to his and stayed that way until he finally pulled away.

"Come on, let's get you inside." He guided me to the front door.

When we got inside, Ryan led me to his bath-room and turned the shower on. He left his hand under the running water, waiting for the right temperature. When it was just the right heat, he turned to me.

"Let me help you." Ryan gently removed my clothes, then guided me into the shower.

He grabbed the glass door to shut it, and I held on to it, stopping him.

I looked into his beautiful brown eyes. "Please, Ryan, I need you."

With only those words, Ryan let go of the shower door, then removed his shirt. Watching, I took in his broad, tattooed chest and muscular arms. His hands slid down to the waistband of his band, where he unbuttoned his jeans and lowered the zipper.

I swallowed the lump that had formed in my throat. He was gorgeous.

"Make some room." He entered the shower, and I took a couple of steps back, accommodating his size.

His hands went to my hair, brushing it back. He lowered his face to my neck, wrapped an arm around my waist, then drew me closer to his body. His touch was so soft and gentle. We stayed that way, embraced arm-in-arm, for what felt like hours but was actually only minutes. I let him take the time he needed.

After a bit, he lifted his face to mine. "Kenna, I was so scared when I got to your apartment. It was like I was going through it all again when I found my mother." He let out a shaky breath. "Baby, you're my everything."

Even with the water hitting him from the shower head above, I could still see the tears coming from his eyes.

Bringing my hands to his face, I wiped the tears away, never saying a word. I was right in front of him; he could see me, he could feel me—that's what he needed in this moment, and the reality was, I needed the same thing. It wasn't until the water started to turn cold that Ryan let go of me.

He shut off the shower and grabbed a towel to wrap around my body. After Ryan wrapped a towel around his torso, he took my towel, unwrapped it from my body, and then gently started to dry me off, and I let him.

I knew he needed to take care of me, so I allowed it.

Neither one of us spoke. We just watched each other.

God, I've never felt so much love. The thought made me shiver.

My body wasn't even processing the pain in my

ribs or my face. I felt warmth, and that was all from Ryan.

After putting on one of Ryan's t-shirts, I walked over to his bed. I pulled the comforter back, and climbed onto the soft mattress, bringing the bedding up to my chin.

Ryan watched me and made his way over to sit beside me on the bed.

"Conor and Finn should be here any moment." It was the first time he had spoken since we had gotten out of the shower. "I'm going to go out and take care of them. You stay here and rest."

It wasn't a question, but I answered anyway. "Okay." My eyelids fluttered closed. "I'm so tired." Snug in his bed, I hoped sleep would find me.

22

RYAN

How is this happening to me again?

I'm not sure how long I had stood in the kitchen. My hands ached from gripping counter, and my head hung low with my eyes closed. Anger, sadness, and turmoil ran through me.

Seeing another woman, another woman who was just as important to me as my mother had been back then—hurt, bruised, and beaten—gutted me.

The sting of the tears trying to escape made me squeeze my eyelids shut even harder.

Visions of my mother came back to me—all the times *he* had laid a hand on her, rushed back. I had buried those memories long ago, and now, they were all coming to the surface, reminding me how I had failed my own mother. I should've got us out of that situation. I should have fought and protected her.

Now, years later, I'm standing here with the girl who is mine, who has always been mine, and now, I've failed her too.

Conor is right to not want me with his sister.

It was one thing when she was in Boston, and we didn't know about everything that was happening, but Kenna was home now, and it happened—he got to her. That should've never been a possibility.

It was too late for me to save my mother. *But it isn't too late for me with Kenna.*

As I stood there, gripping the counter for strength, I vowed I would never fail her again. I would show Conor and Finn that Kenna was mine, and I that I would make sure she was safe from now until my last breath.

It wasn't until I heard the front door shut that I lifted my head.

A few seconds later, Finn walked in with Conor following close behind him. Both had the same look that I had on my face.

Finn made his way into the kitchen to the island in the middle. He reached over and put a hand on my shoulder and squeezed, letting me know we were all in this together. As he took a seat on one of the stools, we both looked at Conor, who was staring at me. We remained in total eye contact, neither of us blinking.

"Where is Micky?" Conor looked around the kitchen and through the doorway over to the living room sofa.

I made my way around the island and took a seat on one of the stools next to Finn. "She is hopefully sleeping. She was exhausted."

Conor's head immediately snapped up at me. "Sleeping where?"

I took a deep breath to keep myself under control. I knew this conversation had the potential to destroy my friendship with Conor, so I needed to keep my emotions in check. And as such, I figured it would be best to just give a direct answer. "She's in my bed."

My gaze bounced from Conor to Finn, who I saw was also directing his attention to Conor. We could both see that Conor was struggling to keep it together, so I decided I should probably try and control this conversation to keep it from escalating.

"Listen, you're my best fri—"

"How long?" Conor asked.

I stood from the stool and made my way to the fridge, grabbing three beers and placing them on the island.

"Here." I handed one to Finn, then slid another across the island, hoping Conor would move into the kitchen.

Without waiting, I opened mine and took a long swig, then proceeded to answer Conor with a question of my own.

"How long have I been in love with your sister?" I asked. "Or how long have I been sleeping with her? Because those are two completely different answers, and I can tell you, the love came long before I ever slept with her."

I brought the bottle back to my mouth and waited for Conor to either reply or attack me.

Finn sat there silently, drinking his beer, and waiting for something to happen—or not.

Conor took a moment to obviously digest what I had just said to him, and then he made his way forward. I lowered my beer in preparation, but Conor walked over to the island, grabbed the bottle, then twisted the top of the beer.

Right before the bottle hit his lips, he muttered, "Fuck."

At that moment, I exhaled the breath I didn't even know I was holding. The three of us stood in my kitchen, finishing our beers without saying a word. All of us took a moment to digest everything that had happened tonight.

Finn hadn't said much when Kenna came home months ago, and tonight, he was also quiet.

He got up from the stool he was sitting on and grabbed another beer from the fridge.

"Anyone want one?" Finn held up his bottle.

"Naw," I replied. "I'm good."

Conor shook his head and continued to nurse his beer.

"I've known for a long time that you've been in love with Micky." Finn twisted the top off the bottle. "I probably knew before you even knew, Ry. I saw how you watched her, how you would always stand next to her any chance you got. I also saw how you comforted her not only when our dad passed but when our mom did too. You've always loved her. Honestly, I can't think of a better man for her. I think I can skip over the *'if you hurt my sister . . .'* speech."

"Thanks." I took a swig of beer.

"I know you'll never hurt her. I know you'll always love her. I also know that you're blaming yourself for not being with her tonight," Finn said. "But I'm telling you right now, stop that thinking. We all know you would give your life to protect her."

Finn dropped his hand on my shoulder for comfort.

"I seem to be the only one who didn't know what was going on, but I'm not like Finn." Conor had chosen to jump in at that moment. "I won't skip over the big brother lines."

Conor stood a little straighter and he looked at me head on.

"I may be learning all this now," Conor said. "But I'm still going to tell you right now . . . If you hurt my baby sister, if you even make one tear fall from her eyes, I will end you." He raised a brow, then smirked when he finished speaking.

I glanced back and forth between them because it was important for me to have them both hear what I had to say.

"There isn't a time I can remember not loving her. Even when she was gone for those years in Boston, my heart was still hers. I tried to fight it, I swear I did, but there was no hope. My love for her was—is too strong." I directed my gaze to Conor. "She is everything to me. I swear to you I will always love her, and I will do everything I can to protect her."

When I finished, my eyes went to the kitchen doorway, and there she stood—my beautiful girl in my t-shirt, her legs bare.

My eyes traveled up her legs and didn't stop until I reached those gorgeous green eyes that I loved, a bright emerald green. She couldn't hide the smile she directed at me. I knew it must have hurt for her to smile right now, but she did, and that made my heart burst.

Her legs began to move, bringing her closer to me, and her eyes stayed on mine.

Matching her pace, I made my way around the kitchen island. I would be damned if she was going to do all the work to get to me. I closed the distance, and when we met, I gently wrapped both my arms around her waist, bringing my face to her neck.

She turned to face me. "I love you, Ryan. I've always loved you." A breathy sigh escaped her pink, kissable lips. "I tried to stop it when I was just a kid, but no matter where I was or how old I was, it was you. It was always *you.*"

I pulled away and cupped her beautiful face in my hands. "And it will forever be you."

The moment my lips touched Kenna's, Conor cleared his throat.

"No. No. No. *No!* Please, I can't," Conor said in a stressed tone.

My forehead rested against hers. I slightly turned, and that's when I saw the look on Conor's face out of the corner of my eye. I couldn't tell if he was pissed, shocked, or relived, but either way, I smirked.

"Okay, listen up," Conor said. "I'm going to try hard to accept this, but if I see you put your lips on my sister, I *will* punch you in the face. This is so gross to me."

Kenna and I both laughed.

I released her from my hold, and she went over to Conor, who held his hand out to her.

As she reached him, he wrapped his arm around her and kissed her head. The tension visibly left his body the moment he held her.

Conor needed that. He needed to feel as if he was the one taking care of her. I would give him this moment. I knew Conor and Finn were feeling the same as me. We felt we had failed her—that we didn't protect her.

Making my way back to the kitchen island, I couldn't help but smile a little. Only a little because I was still so upset about everything that had happened tonight. But now, seeing Conor holding his sister in his arms, I thought about how much we all loved this girl. She was our everything. For Conor and Finn, she was their little sister—the girl they harassed and tortured as they had grown up but, at the same time, loved and cared for through all the difficult times.

But for me, she was my heart, my strength, and my oxygen.

I can't imagine my life without her—never holding her, loving her, having her.

The girl had my heart in a vise, and I was fine with that.

We all claimed our spots in the kitchen, and eventually, there was a long stretch of silence. We were all trying to individually come to grips with everything that happened tonight. It was safe to say that every one of us was emotionally drained, especially Kenna, who was not only drained emotionally but physically as well.

After the silence stretched too long, Conor lifted his head that was resting on top of his sister's and glanced down at Kenna.

"Why are you still awake?" asked Conor. "I thought you were upstairs sleeping."

Kenna released her arms that were wrapped around her brother and took a few steps back toward me. I was now sitting on a stool at the island. I opened my legs and took Kenna by the hips, guiding her between my legs. She leaned into me, her body relaxing.

"I heard you and Finn come in, and I knew you were going to direct your anger at Ryan. I wanted to stop you before you did something you couldn't take back."

I gave her hip a squeeze to show my appreciation for her concern.

Conor kept his eyes on us and my movements,

clearly trying to get used to seeing me and Kenna together. I knew it would take a long time before Conor would be okay with my hands on his sister. Conor grabbed the beer on the island, took a swig, wiped his mouth, and took the time to find his words.

Before he could respond to Kenna, his phone started to ring. He brought his hand to his back pocket, pulling out his phone. Looking at the screen, he then glanced up at all of us.

"It's Griff. He must be calling about Brad." A scowl covered tugged his lips. "That asshole better be sitting in a cell right now."

He wasted no time swiping the phone to answer. "Griff, tell me that bastard is sitting in a cell right now."

Conor paced the kitchen as he listened. Kenna's body started to tighten the longer the silence stretched. I slowly tightened my grip on her hip and brought my face down so my chin was on her shoulder.

"It's okay, baby," I whispered in her ear. "I got you." I kissed her cheek.

She leaned her back into my front, and we stayed like that, comfortable now that our bodies were touching.

"Fuck," Conor mumbled.

I didn't let go of Kenna, but I turned my face to Finn, both of us trying to figure out what Griff could be saying to Conor.

In less than a minute, Conor spoke again. "We'll be there tomorrow, Griff, but I swear if I see him, I don't care if I'm at a police station; I will kill that asshole."

With that said, Conor ended the call and dropped the phone on the counter he was now leaning against for support. He was clearly upset, but no one spoke. We waited for Conor to get himself under control, and we knew he would speak when he was ready.

The longer Kenna waited for her brother to speak, the more I could feel her worry. Finally, after taking the time to calm himself, Conor turned to face us.

"That was Griff. They have Brad in holding, but he's claiming that he was invited to your place, Kenna, and that you attacked him when he turned down your advances. This asshole is claiming he was protecting himself."

It was as if we had all been punched in the gut. Kenna's legs began to shake. I could feel her losing her strength. I immediately grabbed onto her so she wouldn't fall, being careful of her bruised ribs. Once I had a hold of Kenna, Conor nodded.

"Kenna, you need to go in and tell them every-thing that happened." Conor pushed off from the edge of the island. "Brad is threatening to file assault charges against you."

A beer bottle smashed against the wall of my kitchen, making Kenna and I jump. We turned to Finn, who had just tossed his drink.

"This fucker is trying to claim Micky is responsi-ble?" Finn ground his teeth. "No way this is happening right now." He paused a moment to take a breath. "Did Griff see her face?"

23

MACKENNA

It was early morning. The sun was shining, and it was already warm. It was clear it would be a very hot day in Central Florida. Ryan and I were already in his truck, heading to the police station with Conor and Finn right behind us. I sat in the passenger's seat with my eyes closed, trying to figure out how I ever got to this point.

I couldn't grasp that I would have to defend myself. I was attacked in my home by my abusive ex-boyfriend who didn't even live in this state.

I did what I had to do to survive. If I hadn't fought back, I'm certain I wouldn't have made it out alive.

As I was deep in thought with my head leaning against the headrest, Ryan's hand grabbed hold of mine. His hands were larger and calloused, but the moment he wrapped it around mine, the tension I was holding started to melt. At that moment, I knew I could face anything with Ryan by my side.

I turned my head so I could face him. He looked over at me out of the corner of his eye, and a smile spun across my lips. He squeezed my hand. Neither one of us needed words. Our united hands provided what we needed.

Feeling like I had just gotten into Ryan's truck, I was surprised to find us already pulling into a parking spot at the police station. Finn was driving his truck with Conor in the passenger seat. He pulled into the spot right beside us.

Once we were all standing in the parking lot, Conor, Finn, and Ryan waited for my lead. They knew I would go when I was ready. The thing was, I didn't know if I would ever be ready to defend myself. At this moment, I was feeling defeated, and I wasn't sure if I had the strength to do this—to relive it all..

I took a long, deep breath and slowly exhaled, then I gathered my thoughts. I still hadn't taken a step after exhaling. I was just about to turn back to Ryan's truck when I felt his hand on the small of my back.

That was all I needed, the support of Ryan's hand on me, giving me the strength that I desperately needed. With this newfound strength, I took my first step toward the police station. From that moment, I moved with new determination, the same strength and determination I felt only last night. I wasn't going to let anyone take me down. I'd already fought my worst battle and won. I would continue to fight and would not give up.

I will never give up. The words repeated in my head.

Once I entered the police station, an officer behind the intake desk, Officer Cantu, badge 2627, escorted me through a door, down a hallway, and into a room at the end of the hall. As the officer opened the door, I noticed the room was pretty dark due to the lack of windows. There was a table in the center of the room with one chair on one side and two chairs on the other that was closest to the door.

"Please, take a seat," he said with a slightly reassuring tone.

I peeked over my shoulder at him, swallowed the lump in my throat, and nodded, signifying I understood.

"Thank you," I replied, my voice barely above a whisper.

I made my way to the other side of the room and sat on the side with only one chair. After I was seated, the officer offered me a small smile. "Hang in there. They'll be with you shortly."

With that, he shut the door behind him, leaving me alone in the room.

I took a moment to take a few breaths, trying to calm my nerves. My eyes wandered around the room, and I saw a video camera attached to the corner of the ceiling and then noticed the mirror located on the left side of me on the wall. In that moment, I realized I was in an interrogation room.

"Holy shit," I muttered under my breath. All I could think about was how I tried to protect myself, and now I was the one being questioned and possibly in trouble.

The longer I sat there, the more nervous I became. I started running my sweaty hands along my pants. My right knee started to bounce with nerves. The minutes felt like hours. Antsy, I sat there waiting for someone to come in, but as I peeked at my watch, I saw it was only about five minutes.

When the door swung open, two men came in. One of them I recognized from the hospital last night. The other, I had no idea who he was, and thankfully he didn't keep me waiting.

"Thank you for coming in, Mackenna. My name is Detective Richard Bose. This is Officer Griffin Barnes. You may remember him from last night," the detective said.

As he walked further into the room, he gestured to the table.

"We're going to sit and talk with you for a little while," he said.

They both sat at the table, and I kept my eyes on Griffin because he was the one I had met, and I knew he had a relationship with the gym. I stayed silent as the detective flipped through some papers he took from a folder. Once he got through the papers, I noticed pictures a handful of pictures as well. Between the dark, confined room and the silence, I felt like the walls were closing in on me. I needed to calm down.

Finally, the detective finished reading the paperwork and looked up at me. "I'm going to ask you a few questions about last night. Are you okay with that?"

I nodded and said, "Sure."

After answering what felt like a million questions about what happened the night before with Brad and telling them the shortened version of my past with him in Boston, I thought I would be good to go.

Detective Bose cleared his throat. "Mackenna," he started to say, "Brad is saying that you saw him at the hotel last night and invited him to your place."

"That's a lie."

"Let me finish," the detective said. "Once he got

there, and things started to get romantically physically, he had a change of heart. He stated you were the aggressor. That you would not let him go and started getting aggressive, giving him no choice but to protect himself. Brad went on to say that you stabbed him after he tried to leave. We have his written statement here as well as pictures of his injuries."

"Are you fucking kidding me? He's lying. Look at my face. Do you see the bruises? I had to protect myself from him. This is insane." As I shouted at the detective, I hadn't even realized I was no longer sitting.

At some point, I had stood up and leaned over the table. When I finished, I slowly dropped back into my seat, realizing I was probably doing more harm than good.

"Detective," I went on, "I left Boston after I couldn't take it anymore. I came home thinking he could never hurt me again. But he followed me home last night and did this to me." I pointed to my face.

"Mackenna, this isn't up to me. I have no choice but to send both statements to the District Attorney. It's up to him to decide if this case will progress."

"Wait! Are you telling me I could be in trouble for

protecting myself? You must be kidding me. This is bullshit!" I yelled.

"Mackenna, I suggest you calm down." Detective Bose rose from his seat. "As of right now, you're free to go, but we may need additional information. Officer Barnes will see you out."

I shook my head back and forth, disgusted that this was happening. I left the room and made my way down the hallway. I moved quickly, needing to get to Ryan, Conor, and Finn, whom I knew would be right past the doors at the end of the hallway.

"Kenna, try not to worry too much," the detective walking with me said. "I can't imagine the DA thinking this was you."

I looked over at him and just turned away. I couldn't even believe this was happening right now. When we got to the door, he opened it for me and led me over to Ryan and my brothers. I went directly to Ryan and fell into his embrace. Wrapping my arms around his waist, I held on tight.

Ryan's hand went to my head, gently running his fingers through my hair. His other hand rested on my lower back. I closed my eyes and took in the comfort he so freely offered.

"Kenna can go ahead home," Officer Barnes said. "We may need her to come back and answer more questions, but for now, she's all set to go."

"What do you mean she may need to come back?" The deep timber of Conor's voice let me know he was on the edge and ready to take a plunge. "That fucker beat her, and she's the one answering questions? What the fuck is going on, Griff?"

I opened my eyes but stayed in Ryan's arms.

Finn put a firm hand on Conor's shoulder. "Conor, calm down. Griff is just doing what he has to do. We'll get Kenna through this. Let's just go before you end up arrested."

Conor shook his head in disgust but did turn away. With that, we all made our way out of the police station—Ryan and my brothers pissed, and me feeling completely defeated.

24

MACKENNA

A week later...

Stepping out of the shower, I caught a glimpse of my face in the mirror. I was relieved that the bruising on my face had started to fade and was no longer noticeable with concealer. It had been over a week since I had to defend myself from Brad and then again in a police station interrogation room. Even though the bruising had faded, I still felt defeated. I hadn't heard from the detective or anyone from the police department since that day, but I had a sinking feeling something was coming.

I was still staying at Ryan's house because there was no way he or my brothers would let me be alone, and to be honest, I wasn't in a hurry to go back there after what happened. I knew Finn had arranged to have the carpets cleaned and the apartment tidied. Also, Finn and Conor went there to make sure everything was back to normal, as well as to grab me more clothes, my journals, and my guitar. I had only played once since I'd been staying with Ryan. I just hadn't had the energy to play.

Ryan, being the wonderful man that he was, had been trying to make me feel better, but I couldn't get past the fact that I was defending myself to the police. Today, I had plans to go to lunch with Chrissy while Ryan trained with Conor and Finn. Even though all this was going on, we still had lives to live, and Ryan had the fight to train for.

I quickly noticed the time and saw that Chrissy should be here soon, so I rushed to dry off, get dressed, cover the remaining bruising, and dry my hair. It was only a few minutes after I finished my hair that I heard the doorbell.

I ran to the side table, grabbed my phone, and headed toward the front door.

Looking out the peephole—*trust me when I say I would never make the mistake of not checking first*—I saw Chrissy standing there. I opened the door, gave her a big hug because I'd missed her pretty face.

"Hey," I said. "Are you ready to eat?"

Chrissy answered by grabbing hold of my hand.

She pulled me out the door and gave me just enough time to lock up.

"Let's go. I'm starving!" It felt so good to see her.

Well, to really see her.

I'd seen her a few times this week when she stopped by Ryan's, but with Conor and Finn, so we hadn't been able to talk privately, and I had so much I needed to talk to her about. I was sure she was going to ask about Ryan, considering she found out the same time as Conor and Finn. It didn't take long for us to pull into the diner across from the gym. As soon as we took a seat at a booth, the waitress handed us our menus.

While I was looking over the menu that I didn't need to read because I knew before we even got here that I was ordering a juicy burger, I felt Chrissy staring at me. I glanced up from the menu and.

"What?"

She immediately jumped. "Don't 'what' me! I've been waiting over a week to be alone with you so you could give me the details on you and Ryan. Spill it."

I set the menu down on the table and gave her a smile.

"There's not much to tell," I said jokingly.

She wasn't having that! Chrissy pointed her

finger at me and said, "Oh no, there is a lot to tell, so start talking."

"All right, all right." I put my hands up, surrendering. "I will tell you everything."

I went on to tell Chrissy how when I arrived in Florida, and we had the first dinner where Ryan drove me to her place. I told her how we kissed that night, but Ryan walked away, not wanting to ruin his friendship with Conor.

As I spoke, Chrissy laughed. "It looks like Conor is okay with it now."

"He seems to be okay with me having a relationship with Ryan, but at the time it was all happening, neither Ryan nor I knew how Conor would react. He didn't take it well when he found out at the hospital, but I think with everything that happened with Brad, Conor felt that was more important at the moment."

Chrissy lowered her chin, and in a quiet voice, she said, "Conor isn't taking this whole Brad thing well. I'm worried about him."

I lifted an eyebrow in curiosity. "What do you mean? How do you know Conor isn't doing well?"

I had always suspected Chrissy had a thing for Conor, so maybe she was keeping a close eye on him. Before Chrissy could answer my question, the waitress came over to take our orders. I ordered a burger and onion rings, and Chrissy, being a lot like me, ordered the same. We both ordered water to drink.

When the waitress took our menus and walked away to place our order, I looked back up at Chrissy to see her playing with her fork on the table.

"Chrissy, is there something I should know about you and Conor?"

"No. No. No, we're just friends. When you left to go to Boston, I would see Conor around, and we stayed in touch as friends. He has been helping me with my marketing and hired me to handle the marketing at the gym, giving me a chance at promoting the fighters at the gym."

A smile formed on my lips because it made me happy that Chrissy was following her dream and Conor—being the great guy he was—was letting Chrissy work with the gym.

Chrissy went on, telling me, "I saw Conor a couple of nights ago when I was leaving the gym. He was hitting the bag hard, Kenna. It was like he wanted to kill someone. If I didn't know Conor, I would have feared the man."

"I'm sure he was just blowing off steam. I know he is really upset about everything, but he won't do anything he shouldn't," I replied to Chrissy.

My brother was definitely angry about what had

happened. I know he feels tremendous guilt. He, along with Ryan and Finn, feels they need to always protect me. It was ridiculous how they always felt I needed them to protect me. I also know Conor wasn't going to do anything to jeopardize himself, the gym, or me. He just needed to work out his anger, and I'm glad he's doing it in the gym and not seeking Brad out.

Chrissy shrugged her shoulders. "Don't know, Kenna. I never saw such rage in his eyes."

The waitress came over with our food and placed it in front of us. We both glanced up and thanked her for the food. I grabbed an onion ring, took a bite, and smiled at Chrissy.

Hmm. I thought to myself. I think she might like Conor!

We both were digging into our food when I saw Finn enter the diner.

He walked over to the counter, and it looked like he was placing an order. When he was done ordering, he turned his head, and before I could wave him over, I noticed his gaze shift to a booth a few away from where Chrissy and I were sitting.

I looked over to the booth and saw the back of a woman's head. All I could see was the messy bun her hair was in.

My brother is totally checking that girl out. I stifled a giggle at the thought.

I waited patiently for his eyes to move from the woman sitting in the booth to finally notice me and Chrissy. I waved, and I saw Finn tell the woman working the counter he would be down by us.

As he made his way to us, I saw him take one more look at the woman in the booth before he stopped at our table and slid in next to me.

"Hi, Chrissy," he said. "What's up, Mick?"

"Hey, Finn, I'm surprised you came over to us and not the girl you were ogling when you came in," I said.

Finn smirked at me and stole an onion ring from my plate.

"What can I say? She's cute. She's usually here on the weekends. This is the first time I've seen her here during the week. I think she's a teacher; it looks like she's always grading stuff," he replied.

I chuckled. "Looks like you've been watching her!"

"Whatever, I have enough women in my life." He winked.

Chrissy and I both started laughing.

"That's you, Finn," Chrissy said. "Such a heart-breaker!"

Before Finn could say anything else, the waitress

walked over to hand Finn a container of the food he ordered.

Finn looked up, smiled. "Thanks, Jess. I appreciate it." He ended his comment with a wink.

He's such a flirt. The thought made me grin.

My brother redirected his attention to me and Chrissy. "All right, ladies, I'm out of here. Enjoy your lunch and gossip." Leaning over, he kissed me on the cheek, then unfolded himself from the booth.

When he walked away, I noticed his eyes back on the girl sitting alone a few booths over.

"See you later, Finn!" I called out.

Returning to our lunch, Chrissy and I ate in silence for a few minutes until I could tell Chrissy was dying to say something. When I finished chewing a bite of the burger, I stared at her.

"What?"

"Now that you're officially with Ryan and you've been staying at his house, are you going to move in?"

Surprised by the question, I snatched an onion ring from my plate and took a bite, allowing me some time to answer. My silence made Chrissy concerned.

"Kenna, what's wrong? Are you and Ryan not working out?"

"No, everything is fine, at least I think it is. Ryan is amazing, but I don't know. This last week he's been quiet and a little distant," I answered honestly, hoping Chrissy could put my worries at ease.

Before Chrissy could respond, my phone started to ring. I wiped my greasy hands on a napkin and quickly grabbed my phone from the table. I glanced up at Chrissy. "I think this is the DA."

Chrissy immediately responded, "Answer it."

As I swiped the phone and brought it to my ear, I saw Chrissy waving the waitress down for our check.

"Hi, this is the DA who reviewed your case," the man on the other end of the phone said.

As I listened, I watched Chrissy throw money onto the table and slide out of the booth, signaling for me to do the same.

Together, we walked out of the diner. With the phone still pressed to my ear, I listened to the man speak.

We both walked over and waited outside Chrissy's car as the conversation wrapped up.

With a sigh, I ended the call.

"Well?" Chrissy asked. "What's happening?"

I looked at her and then over at the gym across the street. "We need to go to the gym and talk to Ryan, Conor, and Finn."

It didn't take long to get to Micky's gym. Once there, Chrissy grabbed hold of my hand, and we walked across the street to the gym. As we entered, the front desk was empty, but the main room was crowded with people lifting. We made our way to the next room and saw Finn outside the octagon, yelling directions to Conor and Ryan, who were grappling in the center of the mat.

"Ryan, head back," Finn was yelling. "Get your arm out of there before he has it trapped."

Chrissy let go of my hand, and I stayed frozen in place, watching Chrissy walk over to Finn. I couldn't hear what was said, but I saw Finn look back at me.

"Guys," Finn shouted. "Break!"

Both Conor and Ryan dropped to the mat, taking a few breaths. I took a few steps forward. Conor and Ryan jumped to their feet as soon as they saw me. Ryan was out of the octagon and in front of me in seconds.

His wrapped hands on either side of my cheeks. "Baby, what's going on?"

Conor and Finn were right beside him, Conor standing tall and scary, Finn calm as he usually was.

"I got a call from the DA." I looked at the three giant men in front of me. "There is good news and bad news."

"Fuck, Micky, hit us with it," Finn stated.

"Good news: there are no charges against me for stabbing Brad. The bad news . . ." I stopped and looked at them. "You guys need to hold it together, okay?"

"Spit it out, Mick," Conor seethed.

I took a deep breath because I knew they wouldn't be happy. "Bad news: no charges for Brad either."

"What the fuck do you mean? No charges against Brad? You have to be fuckin' kidding me!" Conor yelled, then he turned and punched the bag hanging from the ceiling.

"Conor." I reached out for him, but Ryan grabbed my arm, pulling me back toward him. "Let's focus on the good news. Now we can move on. Brad is gone, and I highly doubt he'll ever try anything again after what I did to him."

"This is fucking bullshit!" Conor punched the bag one last time before storming off.

Chrissy took a step back, then said, "I got Conor. Kenna, are you all set to get home?"

Ryan jumped in. "She's fine. I'm done for the day." He looked over at Finn, and he nodded in agreement.

Looks like I just ended everyone's day with this news.

Ryan walked over and grabbed his shirt hanging on the octagon. Before putting it over his head, he wiped the sweat off his face and chest with the towel that was beside his shirt.

I stood and watched. It was hard not to 'watch' Ryan.

He's always beautiful to me. But standing there sweaty with no shirt and his tattoos on display makes him even more so.

I wasn't sure it was ever possible for him to look better, but when he trained for a fight, oh, my god, he was just gorgeous, and he was mine. At least, I hoped he was. After everything that had happened, Ryan had been so distant and quiet. He started to treat me like I was some damsel.

I'm no damsel. The thought annoyed the shit out of me. *I take care of myself.*

I couldn't understand why Ryan and my brothers couldn't see that. I wasn't sure if they would ever see me as someone they didn't need to protect.

Ryan put an arm over my shoulder, drawing me out of my lust-fogged brain.

"You ready to go, Kenna?"

I turned and walked over to Finn, who immediately wrapped me in his big arms and kissed my head. Before I could pull away, he turned me away from Ryan, then leaned down to my height.

"Micky, I'm proud of you," he whispered. "And I agree. I think you've seen the last of that asshole. You're badass. And don't let anyone tell you any different. You are your own protector, and I'm so proud of you, and I know Dad is also." With one last kiss to my head, Finn released me.

I wiped the tears that gathered in the corner of my eyes. Looking up at my brother, I whispered, "I love you!"

Ryan put a hand to the small of my back, gave Finn a pat on the shoulder, and then guided me out into the hot Florida air to his truck. As he opened the door for me, and I jumped into the passenger's seat.

Ryan stared right into my eyes. "Let's go home."

The ride back to Ryan's house was quiet. I didn't want to push Ryan about the distance I felt the past week. It was possible it was all in my head. I decided it was best if we took the time for the quiet. I pulled out my phone to contact Conor and Chrissy to ensure Conor was okay. But then, I saw that I already had a text from Chrissy.

> Chrissy: I'm with Conor.

> Chrissy: He isn't taking this whole thing with Brad and no charges well.

> Chrissy: I'm going to stay with him until he calms down.

> Chrissy: Are you all set?

I tapped out a quick reply to her.

> Me: Thank you for being so good to Conor.

> Me: Yes, I'm fine.

> Me: Headed back to Ryan's with him

> ME: They're done training for today.

> Me: Keep me posted on Conor.

I waited for a reply from Chrissy, but by the time Ryan pulled into his driveway, I hadn't received one.

When Ryan shut the truck off, he peeked over for the first time and ended the long silence.

"Kenna," he said, drawing me out of my worried mind about Conor doing something he'd regret because that's who Conor was—a react-first and think-later kind of guy.

I love him. I loved that he was so protective of me and that he loved so fiercely, but that was also what made him react dangerously.

"Kenna," Ryan said my name again, and I turned to face him. "Are you okay?" Concerned etched his voice.

"Yup." I turned, opened the door, then walked up the three steps to the front door and turned to wait for Ryan, who was right behind me. Before he unlocked the door, he placed his hand on my hip.

"Let me take a quick shower, and then I'm all yours."

All mine . . . Is he really all mine? Or is he going to pull back further, further than he did the past week? I shook my head as I entered Ryan's home, trying to clear my mind.

Ryan walked to the back of the house, where his bedroom and bathroom were located, and I turned toward the living room. I took my guitar from the corner of the room and sat on the sofa. Pulling the hair tie from my wrist, I threw my hair up into a messy bun and set my guitar on my lap.

Slowly, I started to strum the chords. As I continued to play, the words started to overtake me.

Words of love. Words of protection. Words of fighting. And words of strength.

A piece of hair fell out of the hair tie and into my face. I blew it away and continued to strum the guitar strings, humming the words that were entering my mind. The more the words came to me, the quicker I hummed, eventually putting the words into verses.

The first verse came to me, and I sang it aloud, and then the second verse came, and I began to sing that one too. I continued to sing verse after verse, completely lost in my own musical world.

25

RYAN

Stepping under the hot water from the shower head, I scrubbed a hand down my face. I had barely slept the past week. Every time I closed my eyes and drifted off to sleep, the same nightmare played out in my mind. I was returning to the mobile home I grew up in, reliving the horrible night I lost my mother. I ran, dirt kicking up from my beat-up shoes on the dirt roads where the homes were placed. The cop tried to stop me from getting to her.

There she was, lying on the kitchen floor, covered in blood, but only this time, and every night for the past week, it wasn't my mother—it was Kenna, lying there lifeless.

I could never save my mother—would never save her—from the monster in her life.

Kenna, my strong Kenna. She had fought back and saved herself.

I tried not to feel like I failed her, but it was impossible.

Each night, I woke up from the vision of the girl I loved dead on the floor, and there was nothing I could do. Each night when I opened my eyes and saw her next to me in bed, I was thankful. I breathed a sigh of relief.

I loved her. I had always loved her. Hell, I knew I'd always love her. But I didn't deserve her. I wasn't able to protect her.

Shutting the shower off, stepping out, and grabbing the terry cloth towel from the hook, I wrapped it around my waist. I heard the strumming of the guitar and knew that Kenna was playing. I looked at myself in the steam-fogged mirror, disgusted with myself. I knew I should let Kenna go and be with someone who was better than me, but I was selfish. I had to keep her.

She's mine.

Stepping from the bathroom to my room, I grabbed a pair of sweatpants and a tank. Throwing them on, I listened to the soft voice of the strong and beautiful woman in my living room. I couldn't make out the words, but the sounds drew me from my room to the doorway of the living room. I leaned against the doorjamb, watching the beauty sitting on the sofa with the guitar I had seen in her arms since we were both teenagers.

"You don't need to fight for me, just adore me." Her voice hit perfect pitch, even under the emotional strain. "I don't need you to fight for me. I just need you to love me. It's your love. It's your love that gives me strength. This is my fight. My fight to win with your love."

I pushed away from the door jam and made my way toward her.

Her love and her strength pulled me forward.

Kenna looked up from the guitar, her beautiful emerald eyes on me. She lifted her lips into a smile.

Slowly, I took a few extra steps until I was standing over her.

She set the guitar on the edge of the sofa and turned her body so that she was facing me.

Without a word, I dropped to my knees and cupped her face with my hands. I just needed a moment to stare at her beautiful face. I needed to feel the warmth that she provided. I needed her.

Neither one of us said a word. We just looked into each other's eyes.

I swear she sees my soul—my soul that burns for her.

Looking into her eyes, I kept telling myself she deserved more than me.

Inside, I was screaming. *I'm so sorry I failed you.*

As if she was reading my mind, she pulled away from me. Her smile faded, and she narrowed her eyes with what I think was rage.

I was so focused on her eyes that I missed her hand coming up and smacking me hard in the chest.

"Stop this bullshit now!" Kenna snapped at me.

Even with her hardest hit, I didn't move. I just looked down in shame because she knew I had failed her.

"Ryan, enough! You're such a pain in the ass, you know that?" she snapped again.

I went to speak, but Kenna's hand appeared before my face, stopping me from saying anything.

"I need you to stop thinking what you're thinking," she said softly.

She lifted up onto her knees and cupped my face with her tiny hands.

"I need you to stop blaming yourself for not being there that night. There was no way for you to know Brad would show up."

Again, I tried to open my mouth to speak, but Kenna stopped me.

"What happened to me isn't your fault. What happened to your mother wasn't your fault. You were a kid, Ryan."

She swiped away a tear that I didn't even know I had released.

God, I love this woman. I knew she deserved more than the shit she had endured, and damn it, I would be the one to give it to her.

"I love you, Ryan. I just need you to love me," Kenna spoke softly.

I looked into her emerald eyes again, brushing away a piece of her hair that fell in her face.

"I love you," I said. "I love you so much, Kenna. I'm s—"

Her mouth crashed to mine. Instantly, I wrapped my arms around her waist and took her mouth. As our tongues collided and her warm breath soothed my body, I pushed up to my feet.

My hands slid from her waist past her sweet ass, and I lifted her up. Her legs immediately wrapped around my core, pressing hard into the bulge in my pants.

She moaned into my mouth from the friction.

I couldn't help it. I squeezed her ass harder and pushed her into me, needing to feel the heat between her legs.

Once more, she moaned into my mouth, making my dick twitch. Then, she ground her hips, moaning repeatedly.

She pulled her mouth from mine. "Please, Ryan, I need you. I need to feel you."

I smiled because I knew I would make this woman scream in pleasure.

"Don't get cocky," she said as if she knew what I was thinking.

"Baby, not cocky. I'm just gonna give you every-thing you need."

I lowered her to the sofa. "The question is, can you handle everything I'm going to give you?" I gazed down at her sweet face, and she clenched her thighs together.

"Babe," I said with a grin. "I bet when I remove those goddamn pants, you are already dripping wet for me," I smirked.

"I guess you'll find out, won't you?" she asked with a grin.

I growled, leaned over, then unsnapped the button of her pants. Lowering the zipper, I got a sneak peek at the black lace of her panties, and I growled once more.

She lifted her ass, so I could slide her pants down, and once they were past her ankles; I tossed them over my shoulder. I looked at the black lace panties again, and then my gaze bounced up to her face.

Her emerald eyes shone the brightest green I'd ever seen. I raised one eyebrow and brought my hands to her panties. Instead of lowering them like she would've expected, I tore them in half like they were a piece of string. She gasped as they tore. then she made a snappy remark about me ruining her pretty panties, which I ignored.

My head was already between her thighs. I drank in the perfect view in front of me. I took two fingers and slid them in between her folds, then quickly pinched her clit.

Kenna's head fell against the sofa, and she made the sweetest moan that has my dick rock hard. I brought the two fingers up to my mouth, savoring the aroma.

"Soaking wet, baby." I brought them to my mouth and suck her sweetness off my fingers.

My girl, she could never stay silent, of course, so I knew she would have to respond.

"So, fucking cocky assh—"

Before she could finish the statement, my tongue was already circling her clit.

Kenna's body started to squirm, but I place a hand on her belly, holding her in place. I knew my stubble from not shaving was scratching her, but I also could tell by her thighs starting to clench my head that she was enjoying it.

She was moments away from coming against my mouth, and I wanted nothing more than to make that happen. I started to suck and nip, and within seconds, she was coming undone.

The sweetness of this perfect, beautiful redhead was all mine.

As she started to come undone, her body shook, and her hands gripped my head. I inserted a finger, slowly at first. The moment I pushed inside the rest of the way, she screamed my name.

Damn, I couldn't help but smile against her sweet pussy.

I turned my face and placed a soft kiss on her thigh. When I lifted my face, I saw my girl's beautiful face—all flushed and pink.

"Am I still cocky?" I asked with a raised eyebrow.

She dropped her head against the sofa. "Ugh, you're a pain in my ass, Ryan."

I slid my hands under her ass and lifted her off the sofa, slung her over my shoulder, then took several steps.

"What the fuck, Ryan. Where are you going?" she asked.

With a steady stride, I made my way out of the living room. I stay silent until we hit the kitchen, and then I sat her on the kitchen island. Pulling her close, I brought one hand up to the back of her head. My mouth captured hers in a long, hard kiss. When I finally pull away, she was breathless.

"Why am I on the island?" Her words came out breathy.

I smiled, brought my mouth to her ear, then nipped her earlobe.

"I made you cum on the sofa," he whispered. "Now, you're going to cum in the kitchen. And when that's done, I'm taking you to *our* bed, and then we're both going to cum."

Her body tightened not in fear but in anticipation.

I bring my mouth to hers again and nipped at her bottom lip.

Slowly, her hand roamed over my body, then came to rest over the bulge in my pants.

I growl in her mouth because, damn, her touch felt so fucking good.

My hand glided down her collarbone, and my mouth followed. Gently, my thumb slid over one of her perked nipples, and again, my tongue followed, worshiping her body. Closing my mouth over her nipple, I give it a sweet suck and pop.

Kenna tried to slide her open legs closer to my bulge, but I stopped her, placing a hand on her thigh with a squeeze.

"Cocky fucker," she muttered.

I took her other erect nipple into my mouth and

sucked a little harder. After sucking and giving that nipple a pop too, I brought my face back to hers.

"I will show you cocky, baby." A grin stretched my lips.

My hand was on her pussy, and I slid two fingers into her tight little body.

She gasps into my mouth. I moved both fingers in and out of her wet pussy.

Her mouth opened in an 'O.'

"Are you going to come for me, baby?" I whispered.

"Yes." As soon as the word came out, she screamed.

"Damn right, I'm cocky!

Kenna dropped her head on my shoulder with heavy breaths. I give her a minute to recover, but that was all I'd give her. Taking hold of her body, I swing her back over my shoulder, then made my way out of the kitchen and through the hallway.

"Now what are you doing?" Kenna's head bounced off my back.

"I told you, woman . . . to *our* bed."

I entered the bedroom and lower her to our mattress, then took in the sight of the woman I loved.

26

MACKENNA

Our bed—not his bed, not the bed he said was ours —Ryan lowered me to it and stood over me with those big brown eyes of his, speckled with gold. I took a deep breath—he was absolutely stunning. As he stood at the foot of the bed, he pulled his shirt over his head.

His body is a work of art.

He raised one brow, then lowered his pants and boxers. His hard cock sprung free.

My eyes cast downward and took in every inch of the beautiful man standing above me.

Slowly lowered himself onto me, using his elbows for support. Neither of us said a word. His heated gaze remained on mine. His cock lined up with my opening, and he rubbed himself against my wetness, and I bit back a moan.

As Ryan pushes inside, I closed my eyes, enjoying the fullness of him stretching my walls. We were a perfect fit.

"Open your eyes, baby, look at me" His words road on his breath and blew over my face.

I opened my eyes and looked straight into his.

Lifting my hips, I worked to take more of him— our eyes never leaving one other's.

In this moment, we were one.

His hands slid up to cup either side of my face.

"Ryan. Oh, my god. You feel so good," I moan. "Ryan," a moan passed my lips on a breathy whisper.

"Cum with me baby." He begins to thrust harder and faster.

I close my eyes, and my hands gripped the sheets.

"Give me those emerald eyes baby." He thrusted harder.

As I opened my eyes, giving him what he asked for, we both exploded.

Ryan dropped down with me bearing the weight for a brief moment before he rolled to his back taking me with him.

His arm curled around my back and my head on his chest. I could feel his heart beating against his chest.

"Holy shit, Kenna. That was—"

"Amazing."

We both laid in silence, enjoying the moment curled into each other.

Finally, after I had recouped from the orgasmic experience, I lifted my head from his chest.

"Ryan, what did you mean by our bed?"

"You can't go back there."

My head dropped back to his chest.

"I want you here, Kenna. I want *it* to be *our* sofa, *our* kitchen, *our* bed. I want this to be *our* home." His words came as quiet as a whisper.

His fingers gently skimmed the plains, dips, and curves of my back.

I lift my head once more, looking at him. My lips curled into a smile.

"What about what I want?" I asked.

Without missing a beat, Ryan lifted me on top of him, so we were face to face.

"Move in with me, Kenna. We wasted so many years not being together. I didn't want to miss any more time. Please tell me you want the same."

I placed my hand on the side of his face.

"I didn't want to miss any more time either, Ryan. I don't want to move in here if it's because you fear me being alone or if you think I need protection."

"I will always feel like I need to protect you, but no, that isn't why. I want you here with me because I love you."

"Okay," I said.

"Okay?" he repeated.

I drop and give him a quick kiss on the lips and whisper, "Okay. I will move in."

Ryan doesn't let me pull away this time. With his hand on the back of my head, he closed the distance between us, meeting me with a long, hard kiss.

"It's the multi-orgasms that got you to agree, huh?" he asked, then tickled my ribs.

"Cocky, fucker," I screech, trying to wiggle out from his arms.

The next morning, as I sipped my coffee at the kitchen island, the same island that Ryan brought me to one of the strongest orgasms I'd ever had, I realized I hadn't heard from Conor, or from Chrissy about Conor.

Before I could get up from the stool, Ryan entered the kitchen with a wicked grin, no doubt recalling the last time he'd seen me at the island—on the island.

"Don't start with the cockiness," I muttered, then blew on the steaming cup of coffee in front of me.

Ryan reached into the cabinet for a cup.

"Hey, I asked. "Have you heard from Conor this morning?"

"No, only Finn reminding me to get my ass to the gym by ten for training."

"Hmm, I haven't heard back from Chrissy yet either. I'm worried about Conor. You know how he gets when he's angry. I'm worried he's going to do something bad."

Ryan finished pouring his coffee and came around the island to sit beside me. As he lowered himself to the stool, he dropped a kiss on my head.

"Don't worry about Conor, he knows how to take care of himself. Chrissy went after him, so I'm sure she's watching him."

"How often do Conor and Chrissy hang out? Is there more there that I should know about?"

He sipped his coffee in thought, and finally answered, "I don't think there is anything going on between them. He's protective of her because she's your best friend and like family. Finn hired her to do a bunch of marketing for the gym, but that's about it." He rose and then planted a quick kiss on my lips. "Want some breakfast?"

"No, I'm good. I'm going to take a shower and reach out to Chrissy again."

After a nice hot shower, I was ready to start the day. I grabbed my phone and still saw nothing from

Chrissy or Conor. I opened my last text to Chrissy and typed out a message.

> Me: Hey, what are you doing?
>
> Me: Do you know how Conor is?

The bubbles immediately popped up, showing that Chrissy was responding.

> Chrissy: Conor is okay.
>
> Chrissy: I left him late last night.
>
> Chrissy: I'm not sure how he is doing this morning.

> Me: Thanks, Chrissy.
>
> Me: I will text Conor now.
>
> Me: You busy today?
>
> Me: Want to do lunch?

> Chrissy: I can't today.
>
> Chrissy: I've got a ton of work to do.
>
> Chrissy: Maybe tomorrow.
>
> Chrissy: I will reach out later.

I responded with a smiley face and then opened a message to Conor.

Me: Hey, how are you doing?

After a few minutes with no response, I looked up to find Ryan leaning against the door frame. "You look hot in our bed."

I lifted an eyebrow at him. "Don't you need to get to the gym?"

"Yes." He nodded. "And just so you stop worrying, Finn texted and said Conor was at the gym waiting to kick my ass."

He threw on a pair of gym shorts and a tank.

That explained why he didn't answer my text; he would not have his phone out on the mats. Ryan continued talking as he slipped on socks and sneakers. "Fuck, Conor is going to kick my ass today. It's never a good day when Conor is in the octagon with me."

"I don't care if Conor kicks my ass today," he said, giving me a kiss goodbye. "But you better be in this bed when I get home, woman."

"We will see about that," I replied, then tilted my head.

As soon as Ryan left, I sprawled out on the bed with my thoughts.

Conor has always been impulsive.

The man never thinks before he reacts. A sigh left my lips. *He's just like our dad.*

He has always been extremely protective of the people he cared about, and he'd do anything he needed to for his family.

Damn. I'm worried about him. *He's gonna to take his aggression out on someone innocent—Ryan.*

I was so thankful that Chrissy had gone after him yesterday. There was no telling what kind of mess he could have made. I wouldn't have put it past him to storm into the police station or even the district attorney's office.

Sorry, Ryan, but it looks like you'll be taking Conor's aggression today.

An idea came to me, and I opened my phone and began a group message to my brothers, Ryan, and Chrissy.

> Me: I've got an idea . . .

> Me: Now that things are starting to settle down, and I'm home.

> Me: It's been a long time since we made some good family memories!

> Me: Let's start having a family dinner once a week.

> Me: All of us together!

> Me: We can start next week.

> Me: What does everyone think?

I dropped my head to the pillow and waited for their responses. It only took a few minutes before my phone dinged. I brought it up and saw Finn was the first to respond.

Finn: Fuck yes!

I replied with a heart emoji, and then Finn sent another response.

Finn: Ryan and Conor are in.

Finn: Just waiting on you, Chrissy!

I smiled, knowing we could now move on. I didn't have to worry about any charges, and Brad was gone and out of my life. I could finally breathe and focus on all the good in my life.

Starting with Ryan!

We could focus on being together and starting our life as a couple. And that would start with me moving in with him.

A year ago, I would never have imagined Ryan and me together. I was done wasting time. We had both been through so much, and I just wanted us to move forward together.

After going about my day—planning out the move to Ryan's, writing some music, and reaching back out to start booking some gigs—the front door opened, and I knew it was Ryan.

I jumped from the sofa, ran to the front door, then jumped into his big, strong arms.

Without any hesitation, Ryan wrapped his arms around me and pulled me in tight. Before I leaned in to kiss him, I saw the bruises on his face. I placed both hands gently on his cheeks.

"Conor won, huh?"

"Ha-ha," he said. "You're funny."

He brought his lips to mine.

God, the man can kiss. A content sigh passed my lips. *I feel all the way to my toes!*

We spend the rest of the night in *our* bed. After several hours of us both taking and giving each other exactly what we needed, I placed my head on his chest and listened to his beating heart.

He ran his hands through my hair.

Finally, we're both right where we wanted to be —together in each other's arms.

"So, family dinner, huh?"

I smiled and lifted my face from his chest.

"Yes," I said. "A Family dinner. It's time for us all to move on and make happy memories. We deserve them."

I placed my head back on his chest and closed my eyes, enjoying the feel of lying there with him.

After a few more minutes of silence, Ryan began to speak, "You're right. We do deserve happiness. The awards are next Friday. Will you come with me? I want you beside me."

Again, I smiled. "Watch my man win. Hell, yes. I'll be there!"

I slid my leg over his body, straddling his waist, then pressed my mouth to his.

Immediately, I open for him, and his sweet tongue entered my mouth. Before I knew it, he had flipped me over onto my back, making me squeal, and then rolled on top of me.

With one thrust, he was deep inside me like we were made to be together. My head fell back deeper into the pillow, and my eyes closed, enjoying the feel of him moving inside me.

Softly, I moaned his name. He pulled out, but only to thrust harder.

I wrap my legs around his waist. Arching my back, I could feel him moving deeper inside me.

"Yes, Ryan. Oh, my god. You feel so good."

He brought his mouth to my jawline, then kissed, licked, and nibbled.

I couldn't take it anymore. He felt so good. "Please, Ryan, faster."

"You like my cock in your pussy?" he growled into my ear, and his tongue flicked the lobe.

"God. yes," I screamed.

Ryan rose to his knees, gripped both of my thighs, then he trusted faster and harder.

"Yes. Oh go—"

"Your pussy feels so good wrapped around my cock."

With three more deep, hard thrusts, we both released together. As I scream in ecstasy, he growled my name.

27

RYAN

he past week had felt like a blur. So much had happened.

Kenna was in the process of moving in with me. When I wasn't at the gym training, her brothers and I were at her apartment clearing everything out.

She hadn't been back, and that was just fine with me. I didn't want her to have to relive that night. She had been through enough. It was time for her to be happy, and I did everything I had to in order to make sure that happened.

We had our first family dinner at Conor's and Finn's place.

Kenna was right. We needed to start making some happy memories again. I would like to say dinner went great, but I'd be lying to myself.

Hell, I had watched my best friend grow angry at

the world. He was quiet, working out even more than usual. From what I could tell, he hadn't been able to let go of what had happened to his sister.

I knew Kenna saw it too and was worried about him.

Conor's eyes had turned cold, and like Kenna, I was concerned Conor was going to do something stupid.

Tonight, though, was a night to celebrate. Tonight were the MMA awards, and not only was I up for an award, but so was the gym that Conor, Finn, and Mackenna owned.

Kenna had never expected to own a part of the gym. And she was shocked that her dad had her own it with her brothers. At the dinner the other night, she mentioned she wanted to let Conor and Finn have her shares, saying that it should be theirs, and she never wanted it.

Neither Conor nor Finn would hear of it.

Conor had shut her down immediately. So, Kenna chose not to push the subject at dinner and later told me that she'd let it be for now, at least, until Conor was out of this rage-state he was in.

It was still morning, and the awards were not until later tonight, so I was at the gym getting a workout in with Finn. Usually, Conor was there, but I'd not seen him, so I turned to Finn.

"Where's Conor?" I asked. "He's always here."

Even though we hadn't talked about how Conor had been handling things lately, I knew Finn was just as worried as Kenna and me.

"I haven't seen him since yesterday. He wasn't home this morning. And it looked like he didn't sleep in his bed. Maybe he hooked up with a chick last night."

I shrugged my shoulders, agreeing. There been plenty of times Conor hadn't come home and spent the night at some girl's place, but this was the first time he hadn't come to the gym.

Finn and I both continued our workouts without any additional discussion with Conor. When we were done, I grabbed my bag to head home. I decided it was better to shower there, so I could get ready for the awards. I said bye to Finn and told him I would see him tonight. I had a car picking Kenna and me up in a few hours, giving me plenty of time to get ready.

"I'll see you tonight, Finn." I grabbed my bag and headed toward the door.

"All right, take care." Finn wiped his forehead with a towel.

"I've got a car picking up Kenna and me in a few hours, so I have plenty of time to get ready," I added, turning back to him.

"Sounds good. See you at the awards," Finn said with a nod.

"Definitely," I replied before heading out of the gym.

I grew up in a mobile home park with a mother who was murdered by his father. Now, here I was in the prime of my career, making seven figures and up for an award. The best part of it all was that the woman I'd loved since I was a teenager was just through the front door, and she loved me. At this moment, life could not have been any more perfect.

When I shut the front door, I could hear the shower running and the sweet voice that came from the strongest woman I'd ever met. I made my way to her voice. As I stepped into the bathroom, she turned and gave me her beautiful emerald eyes. I took in her gorgeous silhouette. I removed my shirt, shoes, socks, and shorts. I opened the glass door to the shower, never taking my eyes off her.

I stepped towards her, placing my hands on her hips and lifting her up. Her legs wrapped around my waist, and I pinned her against the shower wall. As I pinned her to the wall, I grabbed her wrists and lifted her arms over her head. I brought my mouth to her perked nipple and sucked, bringing my other hand to massage her breast. After sucking her nipple, I bit and released, bringing my mouth to her other nipple to show the same attention.

My hands trailed down her ribs and to her hips. When both reached her hips, I released her legs and dropped to my knees. My tongue swiped between her folds, and I heard her gasp.

I grabbed her leg and brought it over my shoulder. I kissed the inside of her thigh and brought my mouth back to her heat. I began to lick, suck, and bite as if this were my last meal.

Kenna's hands were on my head, and she was riding my mouth.

Her body began to shake, so I placed my hand on her stomach, holding her in place. I sucked her clit a little harder, and then she was screaming my name. Damn, I would never get enough of this woman. I licked my lips as I rose to my feet. I turned her body so she was facing the wall.

"Are you ready for my cock inside your sweet pussy, baby?"

She didn't answer, so I gently kicked her feet apart, then demand the answer, "Answer me, baby."

"Yes," she pleaded, "please Ryan I want your cock inside me."

That was all I needed. Gripping her hips, I entered her in one deep thrust.

"Fuck, baby, you feel so good." We fit together

perfectly and like always, it took everything I had to not burst immediately.

This woman made me feel like a teenage boy who couldn't hold his load every time I was inside her.

"Baby, you feel so good. Come with me." I brought my hand around and circled her clit, and within moments, she was panting.

Her pussy constricted on my cock and together, we came.

"Goddamn, woman, you're going to kill me." I turned her around to face me.

Her arms wrapped around my waist, and she brought her emerald eyes to mine. "I love you, Ryan."

"I love you, baby."

We finished showering together, then she kicked me out of the bathroom, so she could get ready.

A few hours later, I was dressed in a black tailored suit, a white button-up shirt, and a black tie. Even though the suit was tailored, I was still uncomfortable.

I ran a hand down my face, then through my tightly trimmed beard.

"Kenna, the car's here. Are you ready? You've been in there for hours."

After a few seconds of silence, I took a few steps, then headed to the bedroom. But then I heard the door open.

She rounded the corner, and the moment I saw her, she nearly knocked me off my feet.

Damn, my girl looks good.

There she stood in the doorway. I tried to breathe, but I couldn't. She was stunning.

She took a couple of steps towards me.

"Ryan," she said.

I still stood there, trying to get oxygen into my lungs.

"Hey, are you okay?" she asked as she took a few more steps toward me.

"You are fucking beautiful, Mackenna." She was now standing in front of me with her gorgeous red hair laying softly over one shoulder.

Her emerald eyes had a smoky outline. Her lips were natural with a little bit of shine to them. My eyes trailed to the deep sapphire blue dress that she was wearing. It fell in a deep V that ended past her breasts.

The dress was fitted to her tiny body, with a slit up one side exposing her shiny leg. She turned to reveal her back. The dress was completely backless and fell right to the top of her ass.

"Fuck the awards, let's stay here because I don't think I will make it to the car."

She looked at me, her hands on my chest, and I

knew she could feel my heart as it was about to beat out of my chest.

"You like it?"

"Do I like it? Fuck, Kenna, you are . . . you're . . . fuck, there are no words for how gorgeous you are."

I wrapped my hand around her, leaned down, and kissed her like it was our last kiss.

When I released my mouth from hers, I said, "We need to go now, or we're never leaving."

With a laugh, Kenna grabbed my hand, and we headed out of our house and to the car that was waiting to take us to the awards. As I opened the door for her, she turned slightly to me.

"Ryan, just so you know," she whispered. "I have no panties on."

Fuck me!

EPILOGUE

MACKENNA

Part One...

Ryan took my arm, guiding me out of the car and onto the red carpet. He brought his hand to my lower back, guiding me through the flashes from the cameras and sports reporters, as well as gossiping about the reporters who lined the carpet.

I took a deep breath, trying to calm my nerves. I was never expecting all this. I knew MMA fighting was popular and a legitimate sport, but I never grasped that it would be this well-known.

"Relax, baby," Ryan whispered in my ear, "We'll be inside in a minute."

True to his word, we made it inside the arena quickly.

As we entered the large room filled with round tables draped with tablecloths and full-place settings, there was a large stage where I assumed the awards would be presented.

Ryan and I were greeted by one of the many hostesses guiding people to their seats. She was dressed in a long black dress that flowed around her legs as she walked us to the table labeled Micky's Gym.

When we arrived at the table, Finn came over and hugged and kissed me. The moment I took my seat, I saw Chrissy.

Damn, she was gorgeous in her red dress, but then again, my best friend always look good.

Looking around the table, I noticed Conor was not there.

"Where's Conor?" I asked no one in particular.

I swallowed the lump in my throat when I noticed Finn and Chrissy looking at each other. They both had worried looks on their faces.

"He isn't here yet," Finn stated.

"What do you mean he isn't here? He was bringing Chrissy." As I looked at Chrissy, I continued, "How did you get here? I don't understand. Why would Conor not be here?"

"He never came to pick me up, and I was getting nervous because he hadn't answered any of my texts throughout the day, so I called Finn, and he came and got me," Chrissy answered.

My face snapped to Finn. "Where is he, Finn?"

I saw his eyes glide over to Ryan with concern. "I have no idea where he is, but calm down, Mick. He'll be here. There's no way he would miss this."

I tilted my head in question but decided Finn was right. There was no possible way that Conor would miss this. He had worked so hard to get the gym where it was now. This was a huge accomplishment for all of them.

He will be here.

Our table slowly started to fill up with fighters from our gym, and conversation flowed as well as the drinks.

An amazing dinner was served, and by the time dessert came, speakers started to take to the stage. After several people, whom I had no idea about in the MMA world other than the fact they were important, awards began to be announced. After each award was announced, the knot in my stomach grew.

Conor's seat was still empty.

I glanced at my phone, and there was no call or text from him.

I leaned into Finn. "Have you heard from him?"

Finn shook his head back and forth, saying no. I could see the worry in his eyes.

I turned to Ryan and whispered the same thing.

He brought his arm around me, pulling me tightly to him so that I could barely breathe.

He kissed my head. "Nothing, no call, no text, just silence," he whispered.

My eyes began to burn with tears. I looked over at Chrissy, who had the same expression—a worried one.

I lifted one side of my mouth into a small smile, trying to put her nerves at ease. Throughout the evening, I continued to lean into Ryan for strength.

Something isn't right. I thought. *I can feel it.*

The next thing I heard, through the ringing in my ears, was the announcer stating, "And the winner for best knockout is . . . Ryan Devaney."

I turned to Ryan. "You won!"

EPILOGUE

RYAN

Part Two . . .

I heard my name, and I rose from my seat. I looked into my girl's beautiful emerald eyes, and even though she was smiling up at me, I didn't miss the tears that were forming in her eyes.

I'm gonna kill that motherfucker for making my girl cry.

He should've been here. He should have been celebrating with us, but instead, he had us scared that he was doing something he shouldn't have done or was in serious danger.

I leaned into my girl and wrapped my arms around her, not even caring about the award I had just won.

"He's okay, baby," I whispered into her ear. "I love you."

Kenna ran her hand along my jaw, and being the strong woman she was, she hid the fear running through her. "Get that award!"

Moving around Mackenna, I grabbed onto Finn and slapped his back in a hug. "I'm going to kill Conor. Where the fuck is he?"

As I pulled away, I actually saw the same fear in his eyes as Mackenna's. This wasn't good.

Something is going on.

After going up to the stage to receive my award, I headed directly back to the table because I knew the next award the gym was in the category. Before my ass hit the seat, I heard the announcement for Best Gym, and with no surprise, I knew Micky's gym would be announced, and I was correct.

Finn rose from his seat and held his hand to Kenna. "Let's go, Micky. Let's get that award."

I grabbed onto Kenna's arm and helped her to her feet.

She looked at her brother and shook her head back and forth. "You go. This is your gym and Conor's, not mine." My eyes met Finn's, and his attention never left his sister. "He isn't here, and Mick, you are every part of that gym as Conor and I."

Holding out his hand to hers, she placed it into his, and I watched them go up to the stage for an award that their daddy would be so proud of.

Finn guided his sister to the stage, then helped her up the two stairs, all while holding her arm.

Turning to receive the award, I couldn't see their faces at first, but when I did, both faces were laced with fear. At that exact moment, my stomach flipped. I turned and locked gazes with Chrissy, who had the same look as Finn and Mackenna, the same one I now had.

Something wasn't right with Conor. Something was seriously wrong, and we could all feel it.

EPILOGUE

CONOR

Epilogue...

Laying in my bed with the lights off, the only moonlight that shone through the windows provided me a view of the suit that was hanging on my closet door. The suit, I'd be wearing to the MMA Awards. The same awards I'd be escorting the most beautiful woman I had ever known.

Kenna had no idea that she was mine—might never know. She didn't deserve a man like me. The rage I held onto and the pain I still inflicted on people. She deserved a man who would treat her like a rare diamond, a diamond that shined as bright as she did.

My mind wandered to the other girl in my life,

my sister. Micky had been through hell and back, and my dad would be turning in his grave if he knew I wasn't there to protect her. My whole life, my father instilled in me to protect my sister. I may have failed her—not once, not twice, but numerous times. Not anymore. I would make sure Brad never came into my sister's life again.

I rolled off my bed and to my feet, walking over to the computer that sat on a desk in the corner of my room.

Turning on the computer, I took a seat on the chair that I used in high school for homework—when I actually did it. Bringing up the search bar, I looked up flights. The next thing I knew, a ticket had been purchased, and I was throwing a few clothes into a duffel bag.

It was only a few hours later when I walked off the flight with my duffle bag in hand, making my way out of the airport and to a taxi.

I knew where I was going, so I told the driver. As I walked into the dingy bar, I made my way to the bar and ordered a whiskey. At this point, I didn't care about the brand.

"Whiskey neat," I said.

I watched the pretty lady pour my whiskey and place it in front of me.

"I'm looking for Jeff. Is he here?" I asked.

"Jeff, someone is here for you," she yelled to the end of the bar.

I looked down as he turned to see me. He made his way over to me, wiping his hands on a dirty towel. "You're Kenna's brother," he stated, not asking a question.

"I am," I replied simply.

"What are you doing here?" Jeff asked me.

"How do I find the asshole who hurt my sister?" I asked. "Brad? He hasn't been in here in months."

"Do you know how I can find him?" I asked, bringing the glass of whiskey to my mouth and raising a brow.

"Does Kenna know you are here?" Jeff asked.

"No," I simply stated, taking another sip of the whiskey, and letting the liquor burn down my throat.

I placed both hands on the bar and leaned forward.

"That fucker hurt my sister, and now I will hurt him. How do I find him?"

"Fuck," Jeff stated, "I'm only telling you because that bastard deserves to hurt for all he put Kenna through. He works for his father's real estate firm. It's called Brown, Savage, and Killian's Real Estate Corporation located on Newbury Street."

I dropped a few bills onto the bar and rose from

the stool I was sitting on. I swallowed the last of my whiskey in one sip and stated, "Thanks." No other words were exchanged.

Once outside, I grabbed another taxi and simply stated the name of the firm. It was late, but that didn't matter. I would wait for however long it took.

Exiting the cab, I looked up at the sign on the door and noticed the lights on. I waited like the predator I was. I had no idea how long I waited, but at some point, the lights turned off, and I saw a man exit and lock the door.

When he turned to walk to his car, I saw him. I saw his face. That cocky son of a bitch who nearly killed my sister. The rage boiled up inside me, and I swore Satan himself came out.

I was a trained fighter. I knew how to hurt a person, but I also knew when to end a fight. But at this moment, the rage was boiling inside me.

"Brad," I said, and he turned, his eyes going wide. He knew exactly who was standing in front of him. He had met me and had even been in my home and at my father's funeral.

That motherfucker. As his eyes went wide, my hands turned to fists, and I attacked.

I immediately heard the crack, knowing I broke his nose. I hit him again and again. At some point, we fell to the ground, but that didn't stop me. I felt the ooze of the blood, and I smelled the coppery aroma, all of it fueling me to continue.

All the training I'd had went out the window. At this moment, any control I'd had was gone. My fists moved, and I couldn't stop them.

In the distance, sirens whined. They started off faint but got louder. It didn't matter, I wasn't done. I was no longer in control.

I stopped hitting him for only a moment to lean into his ear.

"How does it feel, you fucking piece of shit?" I asked, but he was too weak to answer.

I hit him again, the sirens getting even louder. I got one more hit, blood flying into my face when I was dragged off and thrown to the ground. I closed my eyes as I felt the cuffs around my wrists.

Stay tuned for Conor's story . . .

ABOUT THE AUTHOR

Ella Taylor is an avid coffee drinker who constantly has Alexa playing her favorite music! Ella is a wife and mother of two daughters. She has a career in Real Estate and recently purchased a Real Estate Company.

An avid reader, her love for the literary world inspired her to create her own stories. She developed the characters that now live in her head and developed a life of their own. Her first book, "My Fight," began the life of heroes and heroines that now have a story of their own coming onto paper.

She uses the music that she is listening to help develop the next scene she is writing. Ella's favorite genre to write is a contemporary romance with women who find their inner strength. Family is first in her life, and she uses the importance of family in her books.

Ella lives in Massachusetts with her husband and daughters. When she is not writing, she enjoys spending family vacations at Universal Studios in

Florida. When her day is done, she grabs a book and curls up on the sofa with a blanket

Deidre
Kennethia

Made in United States
North Haven, CT
30 April 2023

36060674R00165